THE RIGHT MOMENT

& Other True Stories

TOM NEWTON

Cover and title page design by Bryan Maloney
Back cover author photo by Art Murphy

Print ISBN: 979-8-9886702-4-7

Library of Congress Control Number: 2025941447

RECITAL PUBLISHING
Woodstock, NY
www.recitalpublishing.com

Recital Publishing is an imprint of the online podcast The Strange Recital.
Fiction that questions the nature of reality
www.thestrangerecital.com

For Brent

Contents

Shadow Rose

The crowd that had gathered on the quay to watch the departure of Shadow Rose held no collective opinion as to whether she would return. Now that the chronology of those events has become so jumbled, it might be said that she never left.

She was a topsail schooner, with three masts. Her hull was filled with bales of fleece. Had a core sample been taken and examined using an optical fibre diameter analyser or a Laserscan, it would have been discovered that the strands had an average diameter of ten microns but nobody needed instruments to tell them that Shadow Rose was filled with very fine wool. Microns meant nothing in those days.

There were questions as to what she would be carrying on the way back. Rumours circulated. Would it be opium, or silver, or guano perhaps?

The Master knew but would not tell. He came from patrician stock and was not in the habit of conversing with anyone beneath his station. This caused him great loneliness and he was prone to fits of depression, especially on deep sea voyages. He spoke only to give orders, and only through intermediaries. He could become garrulous, particularly about the way his meals were served. He required his food to be exactly centred on the plate. Asymmetry was punished by the lash.

At times when his depression was acute he could become irresponsible, as when he drew imaginary continents on the ship's charts and plotted a course by them. This resulted in the chance discovery of an island inhabited by giants only three inches tall. After this the officers learned to gauge his state of mind and tactfully assumed command of the vessel when necessary, without him becoming aware of it.

Upon the urging of the merchants who owned the ship, he grudgingly agreed to employ a man with whom he could dine. And so it was that Norbert Thornton was signed on as Naturalist. The merchants hoped he would keep their captain on an even keel, since he could not be dismissed on account of his pedigree.

Thornton belonged to the same class as the Master, though he was not of the same means. He came from a good but withered family. Furthermore he had an insatiable curiosity about everything. He had dedicated himself to a life of study, which provided scant remuneration. He sometimes had to work as a tutor for children who did not share his interests. The opportunity presented by a voyage on Shadow Rose with its potential for discovery, and that in addition he should be paid for the privilege, was an offer too good to pass up.

The Master and the Naturalist dined together, twice a day. The Master was reactionary, irascible, narrow-minded and ignorant. Thornton was patient, knowledgeable and liberal in his political opinions. He cared little for rigid elitism and was open to new ideas. The months passed. Their shared meals became each man's private hell, though they maintained a formal and frosty civility.

Another source of annoyance for Thornton was the Surgeon. He had previously fulfilled two roles on the ship, that of Doctor and of Naturalist. He had now been relieved of the latter. In truth he had no ability or interest in the subject. Neither the Master, nor the owners of Shadow Rose cared much about the paucity of his reports or the poor quality of what he did occasionally produce. Their interest in the natural world was only concerned with the effect it might have on their business.

Another man would have been happy to be relieved of the position which meant so little to him but the Surgeon was of a jealous and vindictive disposition. His wounded pride required that he flout the usurper at every available opportunity. Thornton could only hope that he should not fall ill.

What he really wanted was land. If they set ashore he would wander into virgin forests, observing, sketching and taking specimens.

There had been no evidence of land for months. They were becalmed, adrift on a vast ocean under a cloudless sky. The dinners continued.

The Master would not reveal their position. It was a point of contention between them. Thornton thought it was wrong to keep everyone ignorant. They all had a right to know where they were and where they were going.

The Master thought that no one had a right to anything. He considered himself to be the ship and the ship to be him. Anyone else on board was an unfortunate necessity. The right to knowledge was his alone. He would suffer no obligations.

After that Thornton no longer raised the issue. The Master's logic was so deranged as to be immune to reason.

To occupy himself, he studied the heavens at night and took instruction in sidereal navigation from Mr Dawlish, the First Mate. He intended to determine their location. He also wished to continue his study of barnacles but having no specimens at hand, he offered to pay the cabin boy, Tom, to go over the side and see if there were any he could scrape off the hull.

The Surgeon, Dr Foyle, got wind of this offer and in a fit of spit-speckled, bilious rage informed him that should he wish to retrieve crustaceans, he should go over the side himself and forbade Tom from doing so.

The Surgeon had the tendency to place his face unnaturally close to his interlocutor while talking. The man knew no bounds.

So it was that Thornton, with some trepidation, was lowered over the side with a chisel and a specimen bag.

As he dipped into the water he was shocked to find that it was not water. The sea was not the sea. He remained as dry as he had been on deck. There were no barnacles. He looked down but could not make sense of what he saw, just an undefined greyness. He thought he detected motion but when he focused his attention upon it, he felt nothing more than the gentle swaying of the rope he was attached to. He felt a tugging and realised he was being hauled back up on to the deck.

The crew had been expecting to reel in a dead man. He had been under too long they told him. He looked himself over and appeared to be dripping wet. He was on board a ship floating on the ocean just as they were. It was what they all believed, as he so recently had himself. He knew now that it was not true.

At the same moment as Norbert Thornton was hauled back on board, the wind suddenly picked up. The crew rushed off to make use of the opportunity and soon the unfurled sails were billowing and Shadow Rose was moving again at last. Thornton did not share their relief. He was in a state of nervous exhaustion as he grappled with the realisation that everything he knew was wrong. He could no longer vouch that the wind was the wind, the ship was the ship or the Surgeon the Surgeon.

Two hundred and twenty-eight fathoms below them sprawled a large metropolis. The streets were busy, full of delivery carts and stamping, snorting horses.

A man was walking with a determined stride. Large sideburns covered his fleshy cheeks and a lustrous moustache his upper lip. He had a sensuous, curling forelock that bounced as he walked. His thick neck protruded from his starched collar. He believed he had left his wallet at a brothel and was going there to retrieve it before anyone else did. He would be late for his work at Gibbons and Conroy, which would not be well regarded. It was early and the day was already difficult.

The most striking thing about him, of which he was completely unaware, as were the people he passed, was that there was a ship attached to the top of his head that looked like a schooner.

It takes a writer to notice such things.

Supine Tourism

Gladys Weatherman, who had spent many years working as a travel agent found herself unemployed the day when travel agents became irrelevant.

For more than twenty years she had made hotel reservations, booked flights and ocean cruises and even journeys on the Orient Express. She had become adept at helping other people who wished to visit different places and return safely to their points of departure.

It was personal computing that had made her redundant and had left her without income as a piece of flotsam jostled by the waves of technology which swept across the planet.

The world had become both bigger and smaller.

Gladys was resilient. She took quickly to computers. Unable to afford one of her own, she used the machines which were available in public libraries. Her experience as a travel agent had left her impervious to boredom and she spent hours perusing the World Wide Web. She soaked up information and her discovery of dating sites caused her to develop the idea that later became known as supine tourism.

Her market was affluent people. For a hefty fee they could be wheeled to famous sites in European cities, while lying on an adapted hospital bed. Teams of handsome young men, full of vim and vigour, would push them up to the Acropolis, or the

Pantheon, the baths of Caracalla, the Eiffel Tower, Nôtre Dame, the Gaudi apartments in Barcelona, the streets of Florence, or wherever they wished to go.

The bed was sumptuous and could be mechanically raised or lowered. The suspension system was well designed and the wheels had thick tyres to avoid discomfort on bumpy ground. It was equipped with a canopy and curtains for privacy. High quality meals and drinks were served *en route*. An attractive female tour guide was permanently available to provide information about the sites. The whole experience was tailored to individual needs.

At first her clients were the elderly and infirm, for whom such a service was convenient and liberating but soon this mode of travel became fashionable among the able-bodied. More and more beds were wheeled through European cities. Governments were paid off, ramps were added to ancient sites for convenience of access. The Acropolis even became closed to the public three days a week so the bedridden could enjoy the site privately.

Local citizens, initially bemused and curious, soon grew outraged by the throngs of beds wheeled through their streets by the black clad young men. Gladys, with her attention to detail, and her need to be involved in minutiae, had designed uniforms for her teams of workers based on *The Man from Uncle* television series she had enjoyed as a child—tight trousers and polo neck sweaters, all in black.

A backlash developed which necessitated the hiring of ex-policemen and special forces personnel as armed guards to protect the supine tourists. It was noted that many of them no longer even bothered to open the curtains to view the scenery. Cameras had been added to the canopy which the occupants could control to view any angle. The places visited became images rather than reality—a kind of caricature of themselves in the way of old rockstars.

Other corporations had leapt on the bandwagon. One could now take a road trip across America in bed. For an additional fee bedfellows could be provided. At this point the public backlash became social unrest, ruthlessly quelled by the authorities.

The ultimate failure of supine tourism coincided with the demise of civilisation. By this time the clients had all purchased islands or swathes of land and hired their own security guards who eventually overthrew them. The only libraries still in existence were private. Public education was discontinued. Nation states devolved into fiefdoms.

But this is all beyond the purview of this account.

The Monkey and the Metallurgist

I saw that Constance had emailed me suggesting we meet. She was embroiled in a mystery and needed my help. She would tell me more in person.

We met on a bench in a park.

The mystery was complicated. It involved two or more people who appeared to be one, and certain inexplicable changes to the environment. In addition, she mentioned events that had never happened and four doorways that seemed significant.

We needed to go to the Continent. When we got there, she would tell me more.

We took the ferry. The crossing was rough. Constance pointed out a man who walked past us. She had once had an affair with him. Love was a continuum, she said, like a river with a fish in it. I did not see his face. By the time she mentioned him he had already passed us and turned the corner. All I could picture were the sleeves of his jacket and the shirt cuffs which protruded from them, white, crisp and controlled. The sleeves exuded a confidence which I distrusted, suspecting brazenness. I asked her if he was connected to the people who were the same as each other—the two or three that were one, or the one that was three—or four. It occurred to me there might be four. This would justify the unknown significance of the four doors. They would at least have their own entrances and exits.

Constance didn't know. That was why we were going to the Continent—to determine their identities. Then things would fall in to place, for better or for worse.

We took the train to Paris and checked into a hotel in the fourth arrondissement. We had an early dinner. She was effusive about the way I thought, which was why she had asked me to get involved. I was not aware of thinking in any particular way and her lengthy praise was unsettling. I wondered if what we knew of other people was only an extension of ourselves, a projection. In that case relationships were misunderstandings. A marriage that lasted years, and was generally happy could be considered a perfect misunderstanding. Divorce would require a modicum of comprehension.

I went for a postprandial walk. Constance had gone to her room. Within minutes I was looking up at the Centre Pompidou, the inside-out building.

It was still open. I went to the modern art museum it housed. On the fifth floor were pieces from the early twentieth century. It was there that I saw The Dada Head, a sculpture by Sophie Tauber. I had seen photographs of it but to stand before its original three dimensional representation affected me with a kind of resonance. It inspired bursts of disparate thoughts. A door did not have to be real. It could be symbolic and pertain to a mental process of discovery or exclusion. The doors that had occupied me since Constance first mentioned them were not doors at all. This head with its totemic gravitation that hinted at technology from another time was one of them. The question was how to open it and what was on the other side, and indeed what the other side actually was.

I went back to the hotel and slept fitfully. In the morning I went down to the restaurant for breakfast expecting to meet

Constance as arranged. I would tell her about my discovery and see if it made any sense to her. But she never arrived and I ate alone. Afterwards I went up to her room—number seventeen. She was not there. The door was open and a maid was making the bed.

I went back down and asked the concierge if she had left a message for me. She had not. He was evasive when I questioned him further, until I opened my wallet. Then he told me she had checked out early. She had left with a gentleman in a coat with an astrakhan collar and a capuchin monkey on his shoulder. I wanted to know whether there had been an altercation of any kind, if there was any sign that she had been abducted. She had gone on her own volition, the concierge told me. There had been no trouble.

If he was being truthful then Constance had lured me to Paris for some reason other than what she had divulged. This brought into doubt everything she had told me. The Dada Head might not be a symbolic door after all. Perhaps those events which had never happened, actually had happened. It wasn't that I was back where I started. I was further back than I had been before I started. Of course that was a figure of speech and a little too linear in implication for my taste. I preferred curves.

I would leave. There was no point in staying longer, but then I wondered what Constance would expect me to do. She would most likely assume that I would return home, seeing that her absence would leave me at a loss regarding her mystery. If that is what she thought, then that is probably exactly what she wanted me to do, so I resolved to stay in Paris.

Constance was no fool. She would understand that I would stay in Paris because she knew I thought that she wanted me to leave. Therefore, what she actually wanted was for me to stay.

Bluff and counter bluff. I oscillated between them. In the realm of espionage bluffing could move through different levels of abstraction, not that Constance's mystery involved espionage. It was possible I supposed. Its subterfuge and murkiness certainly pointed in that direction. I wondered how many levels of abstraction a bluff could traverse before the original purpose behind it lost its meaning and all that remained was paradoxical. The obvious escape from the paradox would be that there was no logical purpose behind the bluff. It could be bluffing for its own sake, or bluffing for pleasure, or even from compulsion.

I would do the unexpected. I just had to discover what that was. I tried to imagine things I didn't expect, but once something has been imagined it is no longer a surprise. The nature of a surprise is that it has not been imagined.

I went up to my room and stayed in bed for three days. She wouldn't expect that.

I didn't expect the large bill that was slipped under my door and the questions about how long I wished to stay. Constance had only paid for one night.

That was a surprise—something I hadn't imagined. With all my thoughts about her sudden disappearance and how she was manipulating me, it had never occurred to me that she would only pay for one night.

I found myself a cheaper hotel. The fact that Constance was an integral part of her own mystery and that she had involved me for some reason was going to keep me in Paris until I uncovered what was going on. She knew I could never turn my back on a puzzle. My profession as an archaeoastronomer had nothing to do with it. I'd been that way since childhood.

Constance had never been timid. She had always known what she wanted and pursued it without fear or doubt, and she was usually successful. There was only one time I could recall when she had failed. She had said that she aspired to become a novelist but as far as I know she never wrote anything at all and never even attempted to. This was quite unlike her. The best explanation I could think of was that she aspired to the idea of becoming a novelist without feeling the need to actually be one.

Despite her ironclad insistence on doing what she wanted, Constance was never overly self-absorbed or egotistical, and was naturally gracious and generous. At some risk to herself, she had once provided me with an alibi when I had been falsely accused of vandalising Stonehenge.

We first met when our mothers became friends. We were both about seven years old. The two of us were left to our own devices while they talked. She soon suggested that she would show me hers if I showed her mine. And so, unforeseeably at the time, began a long association, never quite close enough to become an intimate relationship but close enough to last for years, at least until this moment.

I didn't know what to do next, so I went back to our original hotel and walked around the area hoping to find something that would narrow my search but saw nothing unusual. I gave up and decided to visit the art museum again but on my way I thought I saw a monkey. A second later it was gone. I could not say that it was a capuchin but it was definitely one of the smaller simians. Whether I had actually seen it or not, this was the best lead I'd had yet and I set off in the direction I imagined it had taken.

Following a potentially nonexistent monkey was an apt metaphor for Constance's mystery. Though I never saw it again, it increased my confidence that the man with the astrakhan collar on his coat was nearby. I squinted at the buildings around me to try to get a sense of where he might be. Not having clues, or firm evidence, or any information at all, I had nothing to go on except my intuition. Then a man across the street caught my eye. He was carrying a *baguette*. He could be the man I was looking for. He didn't have a coat with an astrakhan collar, but that didn't mean much. He might have decided to wear different clothes that day. He wasn't in fact wearing a coat at all but a blue shirt of the kind favoured by French workmen. I watched him as he entered a building.

Then I proceeded to the museum and returned to the fifth floor. I wandered through the galleries until I stood before *Femme à la guitare* by Georges Braque. I had the strong and sudden feeling that this was the picture I had come to see and I need look at nothing else.

The painting suggested that my approach should be cubist, in other words I should examine everything with a simultaneous perspective. It was a confirmation of what I had already been doing using my intuition. The realisation gave me pleasure as if I had received approval.

The guitar, which was small and not quite square, being slightly trapezoidal, only had five strings, which extended casually beyond it into the rest of the painting. Sometimes it appeared to be on the same plane as the gallery floor and at others on the plane parallel to the walls. The cubist woman playing it was right handed. I could tell by the position of the bridge. At first I had thought she was left handed. It took me a moment to account for the flip of axis. This flip always occurred between the observer and the observed, the subject and the object, at least for humans and most other mammals. It seemed quite obvious but was rich with inference and meaning if given any thought. The entire visual world was a mirror with no reflection. It might be different for insects but I knew nothing of their eyes or brains.

Below the guitar were three words in black letters, the third running at an angle to the other two. What initially caught my attention was: *Le Reve* —The Dream, except the beginning of another letter followed the last 'e', and was obscured as if by a fold in the clothing. The first 'e' was also missing the circumflex accent that should have been above it. Perhaps Braque had decided to omit accents.

The obscured and unfinished word was tantalising. Maybe it was *Le Rêveur*—The Dreamer, or possibly even *Le Rêveille*—The Alarm. I felt that if the painting was giving me a message, it was telling me to wake up from a dream. The other word looked like: *Soate*, which made no sense to me. Again, there was the hint of another letter, or letters, following the 'o', also hidden by a fold.

I had the urge to see the room from the same point of view as the painting and turned abruptly. I was shocked to discover a woman who had been standing behind me, who I hadn't noticed. I had been so absorbed in my thoughts and felt embarrassed by my lack of awareness. The woman I was looking at smiled in amusement, which she tried to suppress.

"You can't look at it anymore?"

I turned back to face the painting, not knowing how to explain myself without mentioning my thoughts about the non-reflecting mirror. But there was no need to explain my behaviour to a stranger. She could put it down to one of life's little anomalies if she wanted.

"It's a wonderful painting, don't you think? There's something special about the art from that time. It was a leap in consciousness. It affects me profoundly."

"Yes, naturally."

We stood side by side, silent for a moment, looking at the painting. Then she turned and looked at me.

"You should leave Paris, Monsieur."

This was the second shock in as many seconds. I spoke French passably but was not fluent and I wondered if I had understood her correctly.

"Me? Leave Paris?"

"Yes."

"What makes you think that?"

"I am not at liberty to say, Monsieur."

With that she moved off into the gallery before I could question her further. I watched her elegant back disappear into another room. I followed her but she was gone.

On the way back to the hotel I stopped at the premises the man with the *baguette* had entered. It seemed to be a shop. There were tools and spools of wire in the window display. The man with the *baguette* was most likely an electrician or a plumber. That didn't exclude the possibility that he was also the man with the monkey. Constance had mentioned different people being the same, though I would be a fool to take what she said literally. He might be the same person and just sported the monkey when he wasn't at work. The possibilities were so wide open they were almost meaningless.

I lay on the bed in a frustrated and apprehensive mood. I was being watched, which meant I was being followed. The woman in the museum had been sent to give me a message. She hadn't delivered it as a threat, but by telling me she wasn't free to speak she was warning me there were others who might be less polite if I chose to stay. I had inadvertently crossed some boundary just by being here.

What part did Constance play in this? It was her mystery after all, or was she just a bit player in something bigger? Knowing Constance as I did, I could not picture her in a subordinate role. It had to be something else.

I thought of the man with the monkey. How likely would it be to see someone like that walking around Paris? It was certainly possible, but only just. A character like that, along with some description of him would more likely roam the streets in a book. The astrakhan collar... Now I understood. Of course!

Constance had indeed left a message for me with the concierge. It had been to tell me that she hadn't left a message but had gone off with a man who had an astrakhan collar on his coat and a capuchin on his shoulder. There was no such man.

It was brilliant. She had in fact accomplished her goal to become a novelist, without putting words on paper. Her novel, or short story, was played out in the real world using both real and fictitious characters. She had hinted at such a thing when she told me about events that had never happened. She must have been testing me to see if I had any idea of what she was up to, and seeing I did not she proceeded.

Such a book, at least in this iteration, would only have one reader and that was to be me. I was also a character in her story—the detective who tries to solve the mystery. On the surface it was masquerading as a mystery—a mystery that was not a mystery.

She knew my characteristics and used them to manipulate me just enough to make it work but she also allowed me to be a co-author and make my own decisions. She must have had me followed, and paid an actress to tell me to leave Paris. It was a wondrous feat of imagination and logistics. I think it was always her intention for me to ultimately find that there was nothing to solve.

Realising that I was a co-author of this work as well as its only reader, I decided to rethink what had just happened to me in the museum. Constance had adroitly caused me to spend hours wondering about the identity of the man with the monkey and his significance, only to discover he was an invention. I felt justified in altering the narrative.

***

"You should leave Paris, Monsieur."

This was the second shock in as many seconds. I spoke French passably but was not fluent and I wondered if I had understood her correctly.

"Me? Leave Paris?"

"Yes."

"Why?"

"I am not at liberty to say, Monsieur."

With that she moved off into the gallery. I chased after her.

"Can I ask you a question?"

She stopped. I could tell she was annoyed. She revealed her emotions by covering them.

"Have you seen a man in the Marais with a monkey on his shoulder? He has an astrakhan collar on his jacket."

"No, but I've heard of him."

"Who is he?"

"How do I know?

"What have you heard about him?"

"Apparently, he's a metallurgist from Eastern Europe. He defected. He lives in London, but he often comes to Paris on business. Now if you'll excuse me…"

"Who told you this?"

She hitched up her bag impatiently.

"There's an old accordionist who's a fixture around here. Tourists enjoy that Parisian trope of an accordion player and he ekes out a living from them. He sees everything that goes on in these streets. He told me."

"But why does the metallurgist have a monkey?"

She didn't answer but strode off. I watched her elegant back as she blended in to the crowd until I could no longer differentiate her from the other people.

I didn't believe what she had told me. I had scoured the streets in this area and had never seen an accordion player.

***

This alternate scene in Constance's story was not completely satisfactory, though it wasn't bad for a first attempt.

The next morning I left Paris but I didn't return home to Rutland.

I went to Carnac to look at the stones.

The Jealous Diners

On the third Tuesday of every month thirteen people meet in a private room which contains a round table set for twelve. The place settings are eclectic—each knife, fork and spoon is from a different set, each napkin is cut from a different cloth.

The guests, if they can be considered as such, arrive separately. They bring food with them that they have prepared for the occasion. Their meetings are clandestine and no one else is present.

When they enter the room they immediately sit down at the table. As there are only twelve places, one person is left standing. That person walks around the table and touches someone on the left shoulder. The person thus selected, rises and gives up his seat.

This person is now the excluded one, and will serve food and wine to the others while refraining from eating and drinking himself. Any of the thirteen individuals can only be excluded in this way once a year. They refer to themselves as The Jealous Diners.

The little that is known about them can only have come from the inside. The most likely source is a man from Bermondsey—a convicted forger by the name of Stan Miller. He claims that The Jealous Diners coalesced from among certain patrons of The Turk's Head coffee house in London in the early 1660s, and have been in continuous existence ever since. When members die, new ones are elected. Death is the only way out.

This suggests a corporation, albeit tinged with the occult—an entity with a life of its own. Miller will neither confirm nor deny if he is a member. Because he is the only source of information, he is either one of the diners or his story is a lie. And the story has spread. This mysterious cabal with its unknown purpose has resonated with people.

The journalist, Tessa Walsh, has been investigating The Jealous Diners.

She is of the opinion that they are a fiction, most probably imagined by Mr Miller himself. Yet, because people have been made aware of them by the media, certain unknown individuals have been inspired to form just such an organisation. Ironically, the fiction has become real. The Jealous Diners now exist.

She discovered this when she noticed a short newspaper headline. There was no further information below it.

A potato thrown through a window in Farnham causes £5 worth of damage.

This was odd and didn't seem newsworthy but juxtaposed with politics and sports, it stood out. It was most likely a cryptic message. Using the press to send messages has a long precedent—Sherlock Holmes did it often and intelligence services have been known to do the same.

If one includes '£5' as a word, there are thirteen words in the sentence and there is also mention of a vegetable. This implies a connection with the Diners, as they are now commonly known.

She assumes that '£5' signifies the number fifteen. The calendar of this year shows that 15 October is the third Tuesday of that month. The message appeared on 18 September—the Wednesday after the third Tuesday. Could it be that the word 'Farnham' is not encrypted and should be taken at face value? In that case The Diners are to meet on 15 October somewhere in Farnham. This leaves deeper philosophical questions concerning the meaning of a window—and why a potato?

Tessa Walsh suspects that the answers to these questions will provide the address. She considers the word 'thrown'—a verb which implies action. This could possibly just mean 'go to' the address specified by the word 'window', on 15 October.

If one puts the deeper possible meanings of 'window' aside and just considers the word as a collection of letters, one's attention is drawn to the two 'W's, at the beginning and end respectively. Those positions obviously signify importance. From this one can assume that the street name in question begins with 'W'.

Tessa soon surmises that the street is West Street. There are six letters in the word 'window', so the address might be 6 West Street, Farnham GU9.

She is met with derision. There are a slew of parodies, some of them inappropriately personal. The potato represents her brain. Tessa defends herself by pointing out that since the identities of the Diners are unknown, it is safe to presume that they are of average intelligence, in which case they cannot be expected to have any particular ability at cryptography. Any message directed to them would have to be easy to decode.

Her articles are widely read. She has supporters as well as detractors and some of them regard her as a savvy conceptual artist and social-satirist. There have been a large number of incidents involving potatoes thrown through windows, and other vegetables are also being hurled about.

Tessa has not yet been able to wring out a time of day from the sentence, though she suspects the potato may have something to do with it. Questions remain. There is an organisation that may or may not exist, which may or may not have existed since the seventeenth century, formed for unknown reasons around the time when the experiment of puritanical government had sputtered out, its lord protector dug up, posthumously executed and decapitated. The king had been invited back. He was taller than the average man, and could not afford to hold on to Tangier, which was given to him in his wife's dowry. He was fond of fornication but did not approve of coffee houses.

On 5 October, the risen sun, invisible to the eye because of dense clouds, reveals the murdered body of Stan Miller in a shed outside Cheltenham. He has been shot in the chest at close range with a crossbow, apparently while sleeping.

At this point, another character enters the story—Glassy John, so called no doubt because of his glassy eyes which look anywhere but outward—a result of his diet of LSD and methylated spirits.

He is picked up as a person of interest but is unable to say anything intelligible beyond the fact that he doubts the existence of spacetime. He has three Brussels sprouts in his pocket. They will hold him until he sobers up. But he never does.

What a perfect assassin—a man who cannot talk sense.

The obvious inference is that Miller was silenced. He had gone strangely quiet in the weeks preceding his death, and according to Mrs O'Connor, his sometime girlfriend, he had become increasingly paranoid and feared for his life.

Despite a lack of conclusive evidence, other than that he resided in the shed where Miller was found, Glassy John has been charged with the crime and is being held without bail in a closed psychiatric institution. His befuddled mental condition is a convenient justification for the murder, for his motive could have been irrational. They assume that his incarceration under a strict regimen of drugs and observation may allow him at some point to provide intelligible answers. But this is not to be. Glassy John will die within a few days. A heart attack will be the given cause—unsurprising, considering the state of his health.

These two deaths make the existence of The Jealous Diners now seem virtually conclusive—not the pseudo Diners postulated by Miss Walsh but the version spawned in The Turk's Head some three hundred and sixty-five years ago.

This naturally causes speculation upon what evil motives such an organisation might have and how far their tendrils might reach. They no doubt have accomplices, latent, and indistinguishable from the crowd.

In his book, *Ignorance and Boredom*, Graham Harker makes the point that humanity is entertained by evil. This is a natural inverse response to the effort and repression required to maintain a civilisation. Individuals crave relief from their perpetual struggle against entropy, a battle they instinctively know they cannot win. They seek relief in distraction and entertainment and most often find it in the suffering of others. For that to happen people must be caused to suffer. He sees this as the root of evil, the negation of the beneficial qualities of civilisation, like soiling one's own bedding, or imbibing poison. He acknowledges that the meaning of evil is a thorny philosophical question, never satisfactorily answered. However specious his argument, he has a point. Is the purpose of this murky cabal to foment suffering?

No one seems to consider that The Jealous Diners might be more of a club than a cabal—a group of people in the late seventeenth century, who would meet once a month to share food and conversation. Over time they established traditions, which grew strong enough to transcend generations. Their obsessive secrecy might only have been a desire for privacy. At that time during the Restoration, King Charles II, who had dissolved parliament several times and was ruling by himself, viewed coffee houses as potential beds of intrigue and closed a number of them down. So their sensitivity towards privacy was understandable and reasonable, and besides, no one in their right mind would feel compelled to advertise their meals to the world at large.

The name is interesting. Why jealous? Could it have started out as zealous, and shifted over time, in the vein of flutter-by butterfly? Perhaps it has more to do with their ritual of the excluded one, if Mr Miller can be trusted, which he cannot.

The excluded one, chosen in a curious two step process that seems to mimic the mixing of chaos and order, does not share the food and might conceivably be jealous of those people sitting round the table enjoying themselves. Jealousy, in this case, should be considered symbolically rather than literally—the symbolic expression of an emotion.

The ritual is reminiscent of a more ancient rite, as when a man is elected king for the day and then violently driven from his village, an exclusion or banishment that could be seen as a sacrifice.

The purpose of this more modern version might have been to remind those original Diners that commodities were not ubiquitous and there were those who could not afford a table spread with food—a reminder to take nothing for granted and to respect the less fortunate. Far from being nefarious, The Jealous Diners may well have had a deep moral conscience.

Why was the group composed of thirteen members, a number that is considered unlucky?

An obvious explanation is the association with The Last Supper, when thirteen people were supposedly present and a meal was involved. One might also consider the old Norse myth—twelve gods are dining in Valhalla. Loki, who has not been invited, arrives and sets off a chain of events that plunge the world into darkness.

On 13 October, 1307 there was a mass arrest of Templars in France and the Jealous Diners might have chosen that number to symbolise a restitution of the order, or as an expression of resistance to over-arching monarchical power. The thirteenth letter of the Hebrew alphabet is Mem, which along with its equivalent in other semitic alphabets is said to derive from the Egyptian hieroglyph representing water and this may have had a mystical, occult meaning. Alternatively, the number may have been some form of gematria and represented an encoded message. Or perhaps the answer might be given by a numerological reduction:

13

$1 + 3 = 4$

$4 + 3 + 2 + 1 = 10$

$1 + 0 = 1$

$1 = $ Unity

It is also quite possible that the number thirteen had no special significance at all. There may have been thirteen original members by chance—a number which became calcified by tradition.

Early in the morning on 15 October, before dawn, news teams and their vehicles converge on 6 West Street, Farnham. That address houses a yoga studio. Because the time of the meeting has never been determined, the journalists are prepared to wait all day and into the night. The owners of the studio are extremely upset about the encampment outside their premises. They threaten legal action. Their business has been disrupted and they have been harassed since the press connected The Diners with their address. Someone even threw a potato through the window, causing much more than £5 worth of damage. They decide to remain closed for the day.

Time passes, as it does, and by midnight nothing at all has happened. The journalists decamp and go home. What were they expecting? The Jealous Diners would never appear under such scrutiny, assuming they existed.

***

Tessa Walsh had stayed away from Farnham that day and remained in her office making phone calls. She left early, telling her colleagues that she had a dinner engagement with friends and had to get ready.

No one thought twice.

Hell Morning and Cold Tosh

By Mervyn Hughes, Recital Publishing 2024.

Is this a novel, or a technical manual only privy to initiates? There is a poetry to the title, strident, like a cosh on the head. It suggests a kind of suffering that is curiously shorn of emotional expression—institutionalised suffering.

The book has been criticised as having the effect of a badly edited film. In the opinion of this reader that criticism is unfounded. The story is indeed presented as a sequence of unexplained images. Their flow is rapid and sometimes jarring but the images are never extraneous.

A figure is running through the streets of a town before dawn, looking in shop windows and memorising the displays. Then there is a spate of exercise—push-ups and sit-ups.

Immediately after these violent calisthenics the unwitting athlete strips naked and stands in a shower stall, as cold water rains down on his head. Before him stands an immaculately dressed man with a stopwatch.

The head must be kept directly beneath the shower for four minutes. The coldness of the water feels like nails being driven into the skull. The man beneath it steps forward or backwards, to one side or another—anything to avoid direct contact. The perfectly coiffed man with the stopwatch rewards each deviation by extending the duration a further four minutes.

After twelve minutes we leave the naked man hunched against the wall of the shower stall, retching dryly as he has not eaten.

A gaggle of youths congregate in a dimly lit corridor. They are watching two or three of their number jump over something small, taking long run-ups at each attempt.

Then back to the shower. A large wicker laundry basket is jammed into a stall, water pouring down upon it, ice cold. An unspecified amount of time passes before someone removes the broomstick that is securing the clasp. A man bursts forth, fully dressed, dripping with water and sputtering with rage. He leaps forward and attacks his attackers. He is then taken away and beaten for his unruly aggression. The rod is never spared in this tale. Trousers are lowered to reveal bleeding welts on buttocks. Blood is drawn.

A large bell with a wooden handle is ringing, shaken by a frightened child, who must flee before the sleepers he has woken rise and assault him. He must of course make sure they are awake before he escapes. If they were to remain sleeping there would be different consequences, equally as dire.

The book is filled with moments like these which continually blend into others without explanation. The sequence is broken on occasion by philosophical musings which at times seem overwrought. An image of clear blue sky is often evoked. It appears to represent the insignificance of those beneath it.

This insignificance is used as a relief from pain, because as the logic goes: if the victim is insignificant his suffering is also insignificant. It is a logic most people would consider depressing. It is a profoundly depressing book.

There is in fact escape from this inescapable place. It is found in the deep friendships that flourish—bubbles of love in the sea of lonely violence. It is manifest in bicycle rides up and down hills, in walking through mysterious landscapes strewn with silent stones that are witnesses to what has been forgotten, the orange ball of the setting sun hanging over white fields of snow, the view criss-crossed by multiple dark, leafless branches, the air clear and cold.

These descriptions of nature provide a glimpse of an alternate reality, sometimes frightening—as in the tightly bunched bushes so inherently and inexplicably evil. But there is also humour, as when an overly aggressive flock of sheep converge upon the walkers. Escape is also possible through the use of drugs, usually consumed in the dead of night.

Hughes smatters the text with obscure jargon—*good mob, eight sides, sweat room, shack, shag spot, shagger.* The word *Shagger* is often used as a title, or an inverse honorific before a proper name—Shagger Jones, for example. This particular individual has a predisposition for throwing toilets from trains.

Homosexuals and Jews are persecuted relentlessly and without remorse. Any other minorities, as unlikely as their presence might be, are ostracised. In the aforementioned jargon, there is a term: *Jew out,* which refers to someone being ejected from his place at the table and his food being eaten by the interloper, leaving him to go hungry.

This is only possible through a rigid hierarchy of seniority, determined by age. Seniority is all important. It determines the mode of walking that is allowed in certain areas—whether diagonally, or to the right or left. More generally, it reinforces the structure of abuse.

Those who have seniority are encouraged to mistreat those who do not. As time progresses, these victims will gain seniority themselves and will abuse their juniors. This cycle is deemed to foster toughness and resilience and promote the natural order of things.

Aside from the nurse, who is known as *The Magga*, there is a noticeable lack of women. A few paragraphs allude to them as distant concepts mired in chivalry, or as objects of lust and unrequited hope.

Some critics say the book has no plot, no empathy, no character development. This is not completely fair. The lack of plot is deliberate, for dreams have no discernible plots, only interpretations, and this story has the quality of a dream. There is some development of character, though not to the level most readers might expect. The man with the stopwatch in the shower scene reappears throughout the book as a shade who walks with measured and slightly springy steps, a sadist, meticulous and silent in his pleasures. He is even given a name—Garett, without the *Shagger* honorific.

The last scene in the book describes a winter morning in late December. A crowd of people are walking up to the building where they eat meals. They are going for breakfast. It is cold. They clench themselves in their jackets.

As they approach they see that a long table has been taken from the dining hall and placed in front of the steps outside. Draped across one end is a large Nazi flag, and coiled upon it a bull whip of leather.

Garret is chained naked to the other end of the table. He is mute with fury, and keeps trying to grasp the whip just beyond his reach.

Hughes' style is succinct. Crisp clear sentences are punctuated by bursts of metaphor, such as when he suddenly conjures a guitar filled with water. He establishes a rhythm, both acoustic and semantic, then interrupts it—attracting with familiarity and confounding with the strange. It is at this moment of disorientation that one might expect a new idea.

He withholds as much as he provides. We are not certain what kind of institution he describes, or even if it is an institution—the word is never used. His deliberate vagueness inspires free association and encourages different interpretations, as good writing should.

The story unfolds like a film, a silent film, or a series of imagined memories. It makes the reader assume the role of viewer, or voyeur. There is no dialogue, which only underscores the loneliness of an individual in the throng.

The question is, do we need another book about the human condition?

The Burning of the Hair

I've been compiling a list of politicians, high ranking military officers and officials from the upper echelons of the church, who only have one ear.[1]

I am not including those who have lost an ear through self mutilation, such as Van Gogh. There is some speculation that his ear might have been severed by Gaugin, but it makes no difference in this case as the list is not concerned with artists.

My focus is on those in positions of authority. I will give equal consideration to the living and the dead. I was tempted, initially, to also record hair colour but after much deliberation decided against it. I could so easily digress into the subject of *trichomancy*—an invented word that might describe divination using hair, though I'm ignorant of how it might be done. Perhaps the parting line would be examined as in some phrenological measurement, or the overall shape of a hairstyle could be rendered as a silhouette and studied for signs like a Rorschach image. Each hair on a head might be counted and the resulting number looked up in *The Book of Hair*[2]. Other

---

1. According to Monty Johnstone, these are all people who likely believe in monotheism and are leading the fight against recordings in stereo.

2. An imaginary book which begins on page 75,000.

areas would need consideration too—the dryness or oiliness of the locks, their length, their degree of curliness or straightness. A great deal could be learned about a person by studying such details. Maybe the future would fall into place, maybe not. Baldness would also have significance.

The first bald politician I can think of is the Englishman, or Scot, Iain Duncan Smith, leader of the Tory party in opposition from 2001 to 2003. I recall now that his predecessor, William Hague was bald as well. But it would appear from studying their photographs that both of them had two ears. Of course, either one of them could have been wearing a prosthetic ear, or the photographs might have been doctored. One cannot trust appearances.

A more mysterious approach to trichomancy is The Burning of the Hair, where a small pile of clippings, gathered in a golden bowl, are ignited. At the moment of ignition, with its singeing odour, the adept receives an impression, which is then interpreted. This has to be done by an adept, as hair burns so quickly that anyone less skilled and experienced would receive no impression at all.

The Burning of the Hair has been equated with the Ancient Egyptian ceremony of The Opening of the Mouth. In the early twentieth century the short-lived secret society, Exegesis in Caelo Occidentali, abbreviated to E: CO and more commonly known as The Western Sky, promoted this idea. The founder of the society was the eccentric and polyglot S.E.A. Throckmorton[3], who was fluent in twenty-eight different languages: English, French, German,

---

3. Samuel Edwin Algernyne Throckmorton, 1854-1918, British philologist, occultist and author.

Dutch, Greek—both ancient and modern, Polish, Swahili, Farsi, Urdu, Latin, Albanian, Bengali, Arabic, Crimean Tatar, Chuvash, Finnish, Galician, Lithuanian, Mandarin, Sanskrit, Amharic, Dzongkha, Mongolian, Limburgish, Maltese, Nauhatl and Welsh. He was married to the equally eccentric Myra Throckmorton, née Phlage, first cousin to the Archbishop of York. She was known to be a veritable Rapunzel, with lustrous hair that reached down below her waist, which she wore coiled and piled upon her head. She was a talented illustrator and managed the artistic output of the E: CO.

I have leafed through every page of *The Book of the Dead* (no mean feat, as there are many) and have found no reference to The Burning of the Hair. I can only assume the connection with Ancient Egypt is an invention of the Throckmortons, in an attempt to clothe the E:CO with tradition and credibility. Whether they believed it themselves I do not know. Belief always comes with doubt as far as I can tell.

According to the influential German psychiatrist Werner Jugend, the Throckmortons' interest in The Burning of the Hair was more focused on ritual rather than divination. The burned hair was an offering, a symbolic sacrifice. Each fleeting impression bestowed a glimpse of perfection. If these glimpses were numerous enough one's debt to the world would be rendered void—some kind of enlightenment, I suppose.

The Throckmortons were an odd looking couple, at least in the photograph I have before me. She was diminutive and he was very tall. It was sexual dimorphism at its most apparent, though the turban of her hair made them almost equal in height. It would seem that she didn't engage in the ritual herself.

Interestingly, S. E. A. Throckmorton was bald and had only one ear. The story has it that he lost his left ear in a duel. His opponent, it is said, lost his right ear at exactly the same moment that Throckmorton lost his left. They were duelling with sabres. Both maintained their honour at the cost of an ear. He was bald perhaps, because he had consistently burned off his own hair.

Though he was not a politician, a military man, or a church official, I decided to include him on my list. There are no other names on it at present.

This is a problem because it seems to me that one item does not constitute a list. Even two would be questionable. There must be at least three items. A list such as mine, with one name on it, would more resemble a Zen koan.

I have compiled many lists—of crustaceans, sailing ships of the seventeenth century, animal headed gods, street names that include three vowels, hatters and milliners of various eras, measurements of doors and windows—all neatly entered in journals set aside for the purpose.

List making might involve the same pleasures as stamp collection—the creation of order and meaning, of acquisition and control, all in a general sense survival mechanisms predicated on the fear of death. Philately is concerned with the postal service and list making with words. With its transmission of messages, is not language a kind of postal service?

I imagine that the brain expends a lot of energy categorising things and differentiating between them as if each head contained an encyclopaedia. It's surprising, considering the weight of thought, that people's heads are not lolling on their chests or shoulders.

My concern with list making is to explore its uses as a literary device. It is not usually taken very seriously and denigrated more often than not. There are exceptions. Georges Perec is a fine example. A street in Paris and an asteroid have been named after him, so he obviously garnered some respect. His writing style included lists and categorisations. His descriptions could be excruciatingly detailed.

He was a member of OuLiPo, a group of mostly French writers and mathematicians, who experimented with constraint. Queneau, who founded the group described its members as rats inventing the labyrinth from which they intended to escape. OuLiPo was a subcommittee of the College de 'Pataphysique. The idea of that organisation was the brainchild of Alfred Jarry, who died destitute from tuberculosis and alcoholism at the age of thirty-four. In the same way that the mitochondrial DNA of every existent human can be traced back to one, or two women, I think that the Art of the twentieth century and beyond can be traced back to Jarry. I picture him on his bicycle.

What opinion Jarry may have held on lists, if any, I have no idea. Lists are generally regarded as useful in mundane life and dull in literature. A piece of descriptive writing that is considered dry and boring is often referred to as a shopping list.

I therefore propose the dramatisation of the shopping list:

- One Pre-Raphaelite melon, curved and sensuous.

- Four golden, yellow ingots churned from the product of bovine lactation.

- One sack of cryonically suspended vegetable matter.

- One bunch of fruit plucked from the South Pacific in times past.

- A gaggle of laughing radishes.

- One demure and industrial loaf sheltering behind a veil of thin plastic.

- Two mangos whose parrot green skin promise a nectar that is no longer forbidden.

- Eight ounces of scarabs in a bag.

- A package of sliced and boneless birds, slaughtered so that you may continue your existence in this moment that comprises the history of the universe.

The Chintz Pagoda

Lucia felt herself to be the victim of a ruse, played on her by a Sinologist and his son along with their cleaner, who was now shaking her awake. From the next room she heard the gentle murmur of a voice and the click of mahjong tiles. She got up shakily and went downstairs.

She loved this building, which she called the chintz pagoda, though it was in fact neither. She might have even married it, had such a thing been possible.

If she hadn't met Rudolph, she wouldn't be in this situation. Rudolph was a tousle-haired chameleon of a man. They chanced upon each other in the public library.

She had gone there to do research on Ottoman couture. She was intrigued by the clothing these people had worn. There was not the marked difference between male and female attire that was prominent in the Christian cultures at the time. She marvelled at the *şalvar*—that remarkable billowing undergarment worn by both women and men, and she liked the way they layered their clothes. The Ottoman Empire had been so much more civilised than the hodgepodge of European states and city states, and so much more powerful. The Portuguese had been forced to go round Africa because of it— a voyage with ramifications that had never ceased. That is at least what

Rudolph had said, when they had met and were talking to each other.

She wanted to become a fashion designer. From a young age she had loved clothes. She had been encouraged by her mother, who shared the same interest, and might perhaps have been able to pursue it herself had she not been stymied by the Great Depression and the duty of bringing up three children, which she did well. She was an excellent seamstress and had helped Lucia make the clothes she had designed for her dolls. She had taught her how to sew and had never harboured a shred of bitterness over her lost opportunities, being genuinely happy that her daughter was able to pursue them instead.

Now at twenty-three, Lucia had finished her studies and was beginning to look for entry level jobs in the industry. Ultimately she intended to work independently but wanted to learn the business first, and an income would be useful.

There was nothing like the joy derived from following one's interests. She sat at the library table thumbing through the pages, pausing to examine the plumed helmets of Janissaries. When she looked up from her book she found herself staring into the eyes of a young man who was just sitting down at the table opposite her. There was a sudden and mutual affinity between them.

Before long he had joined her, opening his book on the table and dropping his bag. She peered over his shoulder.

Three men sat together on the floor, their legs obscured by voluminous robes of wonderful colours. They were bearded, with slight and wispy moustaches. She looked closely. All their beards were in the same style, cut short, each one black. How strange to have a beard. They all wore huge globular turbans of white linen and they were holding papers. They were discussing what illustrations were needed for the book they were making. Two fresh faced, beardless boys, wearing the same large turbans, stood off to the side awaiting instruction. They were most likely apprentices.

He showed her other pictures from his book of Ottoman miniatures. There was one that portrayed both the inside and outside of a building. She remarked upon it and how they did not seem to be aware of the perspective that their contemporaries in Europe were using.

Rudolph, for that was his name, told her that these pictures were in fact more real, as objective reality was two-dimensional. That seemed blatantly wrong to her. Who could deny the third dimension? She had been reading about dimensions beyond three. What about the fourth?

In Rudolph's opinion the third dimension was a mere convenience, no more nor less real than Father Christmas. Any dimensions beyond that were mathematical playthings. She wanted to know why he thought that way but by this time they were receiving angry stares for breaking the silence and they took their conversation outside.

When they reached the street, they were talking about something else. The weather was good and the cherry trees were in blossom. They wandered aimlessly, distracted from their surroundings by their ceaseless chatter and the electricity that flowed between them. Rudolph was studying Ottoman miniatures. They seemed to him more pragmatic than the Persian style which had influenced them. He said he was a painter and would one day be huge in miniatures. She could forgive his bragging, attributing it to exuberance. His paisley jacket, which he must have bought in a second hand shop but was still in pristine condition, fitted him like a glove. Not exactly like a glove. It was a jacket after all.

They sat with their backs against an ancient tree in the park. That was where they discussed the Portuguese voyage around Africa. He seemed too clever for his age, which she discovered was the same as hers. After talking relentlessly for hours they both began to feel a mind spinning numbness, a kind of self-perpetuating frenetic motion, or over extension. It was time to part.

They met almost daily. They sat in cafés, they walked through the streets. They were always going somewhere but never arriving. Within a few weeks she began to feel dissatisfied. Despite their mutual attraction he didn't seem particularly interested in her. He never touched her. There was no physical intimacy. Her dissatisfaction began with tinges of doubt and grew. Then one day he surprised her by suggesting that they walk over to his house. She took it as an invitation.

On their way, he explained that he lived with his father. He was a Sinologist, or used to be. He was eccentric. He had become an alcoholic. He slept a lot. The chances were he would be asleep when they got there and she wouldn't have to meet him.

These revelations made her uneasy, and she wondered if this visit was a bad idea. Yet she was interested to know more. She asked how his mother dealt with the situation. His mother had left, he told her, when he was quite young. He might be distrustful of relationships with women, she thought. That would explain his reserve and the distance between them despite their closeness. What sort of woman would abandon her young son and leave him with a drunkard? He seemed to read her mind. His mother had left long before his father had become an alcoholic, he told her. He barely drank in those days. He was still teaching at the university.

Rudolph reminisced. He had been about nine or ten. He was taking a bath one evening. She had come in and told him that she was leaving. She asked him if he wanted to come with her or stay with his father. He said he had thought about it for a minute and then told her he would remain with his father. It seemed a flippant decision, looking back on it now, but he didn't know where his mother was going, or what kind of life she would lead. It was easier to stay with what he knew, or what he thought he knew. Then he would not have to adapt. So she had left and he did not have much contact with her. Now they had lost touch completely.

It seemed a sad state of affairs, quite unlike her own experience of life in which the love she was given, and which she reciprocated, was open and simple. This was the first time Rudolph had opened up to her. She couldn't quite equate his handsome face and his radiant unselfconscious smile with such emotional convolutions. How could his father suddenly become an alcoholic when he had never before shown any predisposition towards it? Was it a reaction to the collapse of his marriage? To depression?

It had happened years after their divorce, Rudolph said. It was after he had retired and they had moved to where they now lived. He hadn't drifted into alcoholism. He had made a conscious, active decision to become a drunk, as odd as that sounded.

It did sound odd. By this time they had turned into Rudolph's street. It was a narrow little side street abutting the park, separated from it by an old brick wall, over which tree branches hung and dappled the pavement with shadows. It was quiet and peaceful.

He lived in an old mews that had been renovated. It looked as if the whole street had been a mews once. This was where the wealthy would have kept their horses and carriages.

They stepped into a large open room that must have originally been stables. The length of one wall was covered with floor to ceiling bookcases and completely filled with books. There were Chinese objects everywhere—vases and statuary—all of high quality, some of them perhaps thousands of years old. There were pictures and delicious silks. She noticed a sheaf of papers spilling out on the desk, covered in Chinese script. None of these objects was placed for effect. There was no pretence. The house had a warm and comfortable atmosphere. Even the light that filtered through the windows was calming.

At the end of the room there was a step up into the kitchen. A woman was wiping the counters. Rudolph introduced them. This was Zhang Mei who came to clean once a week. Then without any explanation, he left her in the kitchen and went upstairs. Lucia might have balked at his inhospitality but was strangely unperturbed. The beauty of the house absorbed her. She stood and watched Zhang Mei work. Her movements were quick and efficient. She was putting knives and forks away and was using both hands. She had a sullen demeanour and worked in resentful silence. Finally, as the last piece of cutlery was put in the drawer, she turned and scowled, telling Lucia that she should not be in this place and should go home.

Lucia was nonplussed. The Chinese woman seemed like the witch or the bad fairy in *Sleeping Beauty* who causes the girl to prick her finger and sleep for a hundred years. She was incongruous. She didn't belong in this beautiful place.

After that Lucia visited the house quite frequently. She came to equate it with the long summer days and the pleasant smell of the trees she passed along the way. Occasionally her visits would coincide with Zhang Mei's but since their first meeting the cleaning lady never said much and quietly went about her business.

****

Zhang Mei did not like her job. She had trained as an engineer and had never imagined that she would one day be cleaning offices and houses. She was taken on at the university and had later been asked to clean for one of its professors as well. In her case the word 'cleaning' had a euphemistic quality, as it meant she was required to look at things and then report on them. She hated being in this situation but had no choice.

Her father had once mentioned to a foreign journalist that he suspected endemic corruption in the local government and had provided some erroneous evidence to support his claim. He had since been re-educated but when she had been contacted and offered the job it had been pointed out that her ageing parents might face considerable difficulties should she refuse. And so she found herself in another country rifling through people's possessions and scouring their toilets, occasionally collecting faecal samples for analysis, far from her family and in the excruciating position of her liberty being dependent upon their deaths. She was partly to blame because of her cursed ability to speak English. The question lingered as to why she had been chosen to learn it in the first place and it made her think that her current position had been preordained since childhood. Life was a trap.

She had worked at the university for six years and had hated every minute of it. Her duties were different when she worked in the professor's house. She was to observe the inhabitants and report on any changes she noticed concerning their behaviour and psychological states. She was also provided with four ampules of liquid each week and told to administer them around the house, preferably near heating registers or fans, and in the bathrooms. She was advised to wear gloves and a mask while doing this. Every month she had to go to a doctor to have an injection. Nobody said why.

She had no idea what the substance was, or its purpose, but she knew it was not benign. She was obviously being given an antidote to a poison. Despite her curiosity it was better to remain ignorant, so she carried on with a grim and dogged resignation. She had watched the professor—once so astute and disciplined, devolve into drunkenness and the boy who flitted around like a butterfly, settling on everything and nothing. And now this foolish girl.

She was indifferent about the man and boy but the girl affected her. She was reminded of herself, and how she had fallen prey to manipulation.

***

Lucia finally met Rudolph's father. He was naked and lying on his back by the door as she entered, with his arms and feet in the air. He was repeating the word 'salmagundi' and giggling. Rudolph told her to ignore him.

Rex George had once been a respected academic. His books and papers were well received. When it came time for him to retire, the university had helped him by selling him a property they owned for a very fair price. Rex wanted to become a recluse and indulge his leanings towards Taoism. He began to associate himself with Liu Ling, one of The Seven Sages of the Bamboo Grove, who considered the universe to be his house and the building he occupied his clothes. Within a few months Rex was a nudist and soon after that made the decision to become an alcoholic. Rudolph described him as a Drunken Master.

As a sage, he seemed authentic to Lucia. It was as if he had transcended the banalities of human existence. He was completely devoid of self-consciousness, affectation, ambition, pride and even ideas—a pure and primordial state of being. He seemed to have no concerns. On one occasion she saw him accidentally knock over one of his priceless Chinese vases which elicited nothing more from him than a chuckle. Then he squatted on the floor and poked at the shards with one finger until he lost interest and fell asleep. He had a strange wisdom. After a while she almost became used to his nakedness. He never left the house and his alcohol was disapprovingly provided by Zhang Mei on her weekly visits. He had a bag of Mahjong tiles, and though he never played the game, he would constantly shuffle them around, rearranging them and studying them while muttering to himself. It was as if he was using them for a meditative or divinatory purpose, though he never spoke about what they might have revealed to him, if anything.

Beyond that he did very little. He no longer wrote, or even read. He slept a lot—almost eighteen hours a day it seemed, but his life of doing nothing left him extremely happy. The alcohol he consumed had none of the usual adverse effects and only increased his joviality.

***

Mr George's progress, or lack of it was of great interest to an anonymous bureaucrat five thousand miles away. Like his East German counterpart he was considered by the few who knew of him as the man without a face. This was because he had made a great effort to ensure that there were no photographs of him anywhere. It was illegal to mention his name and all records of him were expunged. Aside from those few people in the know, it was as if he had never existed.

Over the years, as he had climbed the ladder into obscurity he had developed the idea that the best way to deal with one's enemies, or competitors was to have them destroy themselves.

Destruction was in this case figurative. A more accurate term would be to render inefficient. The idea was that individuals and agencies would appear to function but would be reduced to ineffectiveness. Their ineptitude would be self induced, with a little external encouragement.

These debilities should never be recognised by the subject. Therefore it was important to foment positive emotions of happiness and contentment. Concepts would take on contradictory meanings—confusion would be experienced as clarity, pain as pleasure, fatigue as alacrity.

The best place for this transformation would be where the subject would feel most secure, and where external influence would be least expected—in the home. A cocktail of drugs would be administered. Airborne particles would be inhaled and transmission would also occur from contaminated surfaces, such as bathroom and kitchen taps. The drugs were soporific and produced euphoria. They were addictive but designed to be slow acting, so the desired changes would not be sudden but drawn out over time.

Before being put into widespread use, the idea had to be tested for its effect and the logistics of delivery fine tuned. Professor George had been chosen as the test subject. He was retired, so he would be out of the public eye. Very generous donations through intermediaries made the university useful, and so Rex George bought a house which had been specially prepared for him.

The experiment had been very successful, as the professor, previously so erudite, had been reduced to a state of near idiocy in less than a year, though his decline had been too extreme and rapid. His son, who had lost his ambition along with the faculties of critical analysis and concentration still appeared to be intelligent and function normally, talking all the time about nothing. This was the desired outcome—to keep the incompetence unnoticed, so that those stumbling around the halls of power making inane decisions would be able to retain their positions. Though the initial focus of the experiment had been on the father, the son seemed much more promising. One unexpected consequence was that he showed a marked diminishment in libido for someone his age. He had, in effect, been neutered.

***

Lucia came to the house almost everyday. She had ceased going to job interviews. She understood that her relationship with Rudolph was not going to develop beyond their easy-going friendship, but she didn't care. She had fallen in love with the house. The pressing demands of her future were no longer relevant. She had never felt so contented. She enjoyed the languorous summer afternoons dozing on the sofa, free of dreams. She no longer gave a thought to Rudolph and Rex, wherever they may have been.

She awoke to find Zhang Mei leaning over her, talking in her curt, abbreviated style. She kept telling her to get up and leave. These people were no good. She must leave and never come back. She had no idea of the danger she was in.

Zhang Mei's relentless nagging roused her from her torpor, and if just to escape it she found herself stumbling down the stairs and outside into the warm afternoon. She heard the door snap shut behind her and the bolts being thrown.

She felt jilted, wrenched away from her happiness. The building she loved had been stolen away from her by another woman. Rudolph and his father were in cahoots with Zhang Mei no doubt. They must have acted that way because of jealousy. The building loved her more than it did them. In their eyes it had been unfaithful.

She found her way back home and went up to her room, stricken with pangs of anger and sadness. She ignored her mother's worried entreaties and offers of food.

The next day she returned to the mews but the love of her life had been destroyed by fire. The remains of the building were cordoned off and there were police cars outside. She kept walking, her heart palpitating.

She didn't know where to go.

The Consciousness of Things

"I am a translator by profession. I translate books from English to English."

The sun was setting, filling the western region of the sky with a creeping beauty.

"Do you edit the text to improve upon it, or to correct errors?"

"I do not. A good translator will stay true to the original as far as possible. I therefore copy the text exactly as written and am proud to say that my translations are perfect."

"What is the need for such translations, if that is indeed what they are?"

"What is the need for anything? A text is written and then translated. There is an effect upon the brain, or within it if you prefer."

A murmuring could be heard from beyond the trees. A flock of talking birds was approaching.

"You know, I haven't seen my legs for a few days."

"Where are they?"

"Out walking. They take off from time to time."

The chairs upon which they sat, perked up at this information, legs being a subject of particular interest.

"What would you say is the length of stride of that person who is sitting on you?"

"I imagine it averages between twenty-four to thirty inches."

"It would depend on whether the legs were going up or down an incline, or walking on level ground, don't you think?"

"Yes, of course. That's why I'm expressing it as an average."

The air, which was ubiquitous in this part of the atmosphere could not refrain from eavesdropping. It heard everything, an ability that sometimes became tiresome because there was no respite.

Within the air invisible droplets of water competed for attention. The evening drew on into night. An ant was making its way home.

The Drawing Room

It was a gloomy evening in early winter. The chill and damp made their way in through gaps and crevices in the old French doors, even though the curtains were drawn. At that time there was no heating in the house except for a few gas fires and an old coal stove in the kitchen.

It was a strange name for a room—the drawing room, and seemingly implied a place to go and sketch. At some point I discovered that drawing in this case was an abbreviation. What it really meant was withdrawing—the withdrawing room. It was a place to where women once withdrew.

But these thoughts are all in hindsight. I was about four years old then.

I was with Rita. She was moody. We were waiting for some people who were coming to pick her up. She was going out that night. I could feel her impatience. The house was quiet.

Rita looked after me. She was an au pair girl. She lived in a room upstairs. My brother would sometimes wake her in the morning by pouring water on her. She would splutter with rage. She must have been seventeen or eighteen.

I don't think she was particularly interested in looking after me. It was just a job. She was listless. Something unknown out there awaited her that night as far as I could tell. I didn't find her as attractive as the Scandinavian girls, Inge and Kirsten, who had looked after me before. No one could compare to Inge. Even at three years old I was madly in love with her. I remember nothing more about her now, except that she existed once, but her warmth still finds its way through my forgetfulness.

There was an emptiness to the drawing room. It was not due to a lack of furniture. There were two armchairs, a side table or two, an old Chesterfield sofa, a piano, a Braun radiogram and a red carpet. The Braun was the height of German engineering and technology, a radio and record player contained in a hefty cabinet of blond birch. There was a fireplace surrounded by an elaborate mantelpiece in which a fire never burned.

Within a few years I became very enamoured of the Braun. The turntable had four speeds, controlled by a switch—16, 33, 45 and 78. I would slather my hair with Vaseline and play Elvis Presley 45s, while singing along. I'd drop the speed to 16 for "I'm in love" then ramp it up to 78 for "I'm all shook up", which I would sing as: "I'm all greased up". It took days of shampooing to get the Vaseline out. I learned the speed changing trick from my brother who taught me most of what I knew.

The emptiness, not being due to a lack of furniture was psychological, or emotional in nature. It was a kind of perverse nostalgia which yearned for a past that had never quite happened. It had a constrictive effect—any dream of becoming someone, any idea of achievement and success in society, any experience of unselfconscious fun was impossible. Only other people could do such things. With it was an undercurrent of snobbishness, rarely mentioned, which seemed to imply that only people who had a certain kind of intellectual superiority were able to sacrifice their happiness for no good reason. Those who were able to accomplish things had a vulgar lack of refinement. The end result of this was a static frustration that stayed with one for life. As a four-year-old I would not have described it this way but I understood. That was why I would beat my head against the wall as a baby. None of this could be considered as suffering, because only other people suffered.

That emptiness was not limited to the drawing room but permeated the entire house and beyond, with a few exceptions. The bluebell patch at the bottom of the garden inspired a glowing wonder and sense of mysterious possibility. It was a place where diminutive beings from other dimensions lived, though I don't remember ever having seen any.

Another exception was in the drawing room itself, underneath the piano when my father hammered out Rachmaninov or Scriabin, which he did quite frequently.

The sounds I heard beneath the piano were unlike any I heard elsewhere. A torrent of notes left no room for emptiness, or even the memory of such a state. The notes were slightly shorn of their higher frequencies and resonated into each other with storm clouds of reverberation, accompanied by the clicking of the damper pedal. The melodies they formed expressed emotions of romanticism so exquisite it was almost unbearable. There was sadness and beauty, resignation and heroic fortitude, tragedies contained in clusters, bursts of rage and love so deep and mournful, so courageous and forlorn.

The doorbell rang. Rita had sent my brother out to the sweet shop to buy her cigarettes and I thought it might be him but moments later four men came into the drawing room.

I was awestruck. I stood looking up at them. The one that most caught my attention had the blondest of blond hair. He was the one Rita was waiting for and I learned his name was Heinz.

He must have said something to me as I stood before him in silence, but if he did I can no longer remember.

They all wore black leather jackets. There was a connection between them, a confidence and shared purpose more powerful than friendship. They were a band of warriors. For them emptiness was nothing.

I found out later that they were in fact a band—a pop group called the Tornados, and they had a hit single at the time with their instrumental Telstar.

Unaware of that as I craned my neck up to Heinz's handsome face and basked in his presence, I was filled with an instant certitude.

This was what I would be.

The Sun Rose on Word Street

The inamoratas crossed over the mountain and came down into the valley.

The valley, a cleft carved by a glacier in distant times, was filled with the sound of traffic.

They paused, the barren beauty of the mountain at their backs. There were nine of them, each one leaving an old life behind. Nothing much grew on the other side of the mountain, which was why they had crossed it.

The town was full of bee keepers and long distance runners. Once a year the sun rose at the end of Word Street and beamed its rays straight down the thoroughfare. The exact time of this event changed slightly from year to year due to the precession of the equinoxes, which caused the perceived motion of the sun on the ecliptic. It would occur at the same time once every twenty-five thousand seven hundred years.

Anyone touched by that light was transformed. It turned shopkeepers into poets, cantankerous old codgers into gallant lovers. It turned minutes to seconds and hours to years. Word Street was always packed with a crowd that day, shoulder to shoulder, waiting to be bathed in the morning light.

Woe betide anyone who tried to take a photograph. The consequence of that was severe. Its effect was similar to the tale of the wind changing, and would etch upon a face a grimace that lasted for life.

Lifting the Television

I moved a television for a psychic. At that time television sets were cathode ray tubes encased in hefty boxes with curved glass screens. She wasn't able to handle it herself.

She lived in Little Italy, not far from my place in Soho. I walked over to her apartment. A biting wind cut through the streets.

We had never met before but she seemed to know who I was. She was barely twice the height of her television set. I could see why she needed help with it. We had an agreement. I would put the television wherever she wanted it and she would give me a viewing.

That was the way she looked into the future—by watching television. She had apparently seen films that had not yet been made.

She was nervous as I staggered across her apartment with it. This was her livelihood. No other television would do. When I carried the thing it reached from my groin almost to my chin. She talked incessantly, telling me that a few weeks earlier she had watched a cartoon in which I had hurt my left arm. She kept asking me to be careful, which wasn't helpful but before too long, and without mishap, the television was where she wanted it.

I wondered if when she sat alone watching the future, she regarded it as entertainment, or whether she considered it as work and studied each scene for meaning. I found the future as entertainment a more interesting idea. I would have liked to see what she watched.

She had a lucrative business. Most of her clients were from the aristocracy of the avant-garde and they all spoke highly of her—they swore by her. It made me feel that this waif-like woman controlled the pulse of the city, or had her finger on it. She gave me the impression that she tolerated no nonsense and now that the heavy lifting was done there was no necessity for my continued presence. She told me to come back the next day and she would tell me what she had seen. I should leave a message with her answering service first. She could have paid me in cash, she wasn't short of it, but she seemed to think a viewing would be worth more to me than money, and that she was doing me a special favour.

I was the one doing her a favour. I hadn't really wanted to move the television anyway, and I wasn't interested in psychic viewings or readings. What was to be gained from knowing the future if it could not be changed? Life would be a state of dread or constant anticipation. And if she could indeed see the future, then it would have to be unchangeable, as otherwise it would not be the future, just something she had thought up for money. I supposed it was possible that she might have been watching probabilities and not an immutable future—then her gazing into the crystal box would have a different significance.

I made my way west across Prince Street to Fanelli's. I had a book in my pocket—*Grammatical Man*[1] . There was a large

---

1. Grammatical Man by Jeremy Campbell, Simon & Schuster 1982.

old wood stove in the back room that generated a lot of heat. I wanted to sit there with a glass of wine and read my book. *Grammatical Man* was about information theory, probability, entropy, linguistics and cybernetics. At that time, in the early 1980s, the concept of information as a science was seeping into the popular consciousness and these ideas were just as mysterious to me as the future revealed on a television.

I was fascinated by redundancy in language, and its importance for the successful transmission of messages. If I took the vowels out of my name, I could still recognise it and someone who knew me probably would too, but a stranger might not know it was a name and see it only as a jumble of consonants. I imagined removing the letters from a book, one by one, and counting how many it took to cross the threshold of incomprehensibility.

Cybernetics seemed mostly concerned with feedback loops—plugging the output back into the input. There were all kinds of applications for that—car engines and conversations for example.

But then there was feedforward.

When my eyes first set upon that word I was filled with a mild disgust, suspecting it to be a kind of newspeak that exemplified the denial of the chthonic beauty of language. But then I realised that I didn't have the same emotional bias against the word 'feedback', presumably because I was familiar with it. I was perhaps more conservative in my aesthetic tastes than I had thought. It was disturbing, but my doubts were soon dispelled by the meaning of the word.

It described the context of planning for the outcome of feedback, measuring disturbances at the input, not the output. The term had been assimilated into cybernetics and had spread into other disciplines. In behavioural psychology it was considered to be a way to learn from the future. I liked that idea, because it affirmed my desire to hold the opinion that the distinctions between past, present and future were arbitrary, being just measurements. They might as well be the same thing. I suspected, however, that what was intended was to bring about change in oneself by imagining what one could be in the future, in other words through creative visualisation. It was disappointing. I much preferred improvement by learning from unexperienced experiences. It was more profound. There was something annoying about creative visualisation. It was like praying for consumer goods.

After I had left Fanelli's and was walking back home down Mercer Street, clenching myself against the bitter cold, the warmth of wine and the wood stove just a memory, I noticed that I had a severe pain in my arm and a numbness in my hand. I had obviously pulled a muscle or damaged a tendon lifting that monstrous television. But she was right—it was my left arm.

It had not improved when I got up the next day, so I went to the walk-in clinic on Spring Street, where a doctor with a cigarette dangling from his lips gave me a vitamin B injection. I was not really sure why he did that. Some things must remain inexplicable.

I found a pay phone that worked and left a message with her answering service that I was on my way. Having learned about the concept of feedforward I was quite excited to hear what she had seen. I might even be able to learn from the future. I kept thinking about how she said she had seen me in a cartoon. What did that mean? Cartoon characters could suffer repeated amounts of physical trauma and never suffer pain. This, I supposed, was the advantage of being an animation in a two dimensional world. Was I a cartoon character? The pain in my arm seemed real enough.

When I reached her tenement on Elizabeth Street and rang her bell, she came down to meet me and didn't invite me in.

"Thanks for moving the TV. I saw a show about you last night. It seems you're going to be the father of two children. You have some artistic ability in music and writing, but not much will come of it."

This seemed remarkably underwhelming, barely worth the weight I had lifted. There was little I could think of learning from that kind of future. I expected more but nothing was forthcoming.

"Is that it?"

"Yes."

"Tell me, did you see this in a cartoon?"

"No. It was a western. Im not usually into that kind of thing but it was actually pretty good."

Malarkey and Abdul

Malarkey was a dog lover with a mischievous glint in his eye, who was much beloved by children for his amusing tricks and jokes. He would run around with an empty paper bag, gazing upwards as if looking at something that was falling and with much contortion and physical gyration he would manage to catch it, giving credence to the non-existent object by surreptitiously flicking the bag with his thumb at the correct moment of its imaginary entry.

This game, seemingly so innocent and good natured, produced laughter and wonderment in children but had a deeper meaning.

Abdul was a kind man. He used to have an eye for fashion when he was young—wearing tight trousers, turned up at the ankle in casual perfection and shoes with thick crepe soles. He was not morally developed at the time and was able to shoplift without remorse, always generous with the proceeds and dressing his friends in style.

He had thickened over the years from good food, provided by his mother and his wife. Unbeknownst to both of them, he had a secret collection of garden gnomes, hidden among bluebell patches and gooseberry bushes. They all had conical hats, some flopped over to the side. They embarrassed him. He had always been aware of their significance but feared being mocked as different.

The two names Malarkey and Abdul, which might just as easily have been Hutchins and Broadbent—and like the pop groups that began to flourish in the West after The Second World War, implied a male bond founded upon a shared purpose. It was an evolution of what an anthropologist might have described as a hunting band. Modernity could hijack the primitive.

James Malarkey and Tariq Abdul both worked as pilots for a commercial airline.

***

Their flight was routine, cruising at forty thousand feet, at a speed of five hundred and eighty miles an hour with a tailwind. There was some turbulence as Malarkey began the descent and Abdul switched on the seatbelt signs. They pierced the clouds and lost visibility.

Then they lost radio contact.

This was a situation he had not faced before but Malarkey remained calm—a calmness bordering on panic. He knew he had a very short time to make a decision. They had not been cleared for landing. He could only hope that there were no other planes in the vicinity. He was flying by instruments. The cloud cover was dense and seemed to reach much lower to the ground than usual. Then he saw dim lights below him, runway lights.

"I'm taking her down, Tariq. This may be it."

Lost in his own fear, Abdul said nothing but tightened his seat belt. There was no sound but the noise of the engines, relentless and powerful.

The fog thinned as the ground approached. The runway was lined by naked flames. The port wheel touched down first and the aircraft shuddered. A sickening second passed, then all the wheels were down and the engines roared, the ailerons up and straining. They hurtled down the runway, their momentum an act against nature.

Their relief soon subsided as they looked out at their surroundings. The runway lights were burning torches, behind which stood figures of twigs and straw with faces of painted wood. Each one was adorned with a necklace of shells.

Abdul unstrapped his belt.

"I'm going back to check on things."

Malarkey stayed in his seat, gazing out at the runway which was not tarmac but looked like hard clay or packed earth.

Abdul came back into the cockpit.

"The plane's empty."

"What do you mean, empty?"

"No crew or passengers. They've gone."

"Are the doors open?"

"They're locked."

"Impossible."

As he stared at the long line of fetishes behind the torches, Abdul realised that they had an existence beyond their physical representation, just like his garden gnomes.

"Impossible, yes, but true. What now?"

Malarkey raised himself from his seat, "Let's go back together and check everything again."

He wanted to see for himself, to get his own confirmation. It wasn't that he mistrusted Tariq, they had been close friends since they were teenagers—there was no one he trusted more. They had met when they both worked in a fast-food restaurant, and Tariq had dressed him to the nines. Later, it was he who had suggested they both go to flight school. Tariq had helped him too, especially at the time of his divorce. They had chipped away at the world together.

They walked back through the aircraft. As Abdul had said, the doors were all locked. They checked some of the overhead racks. Each one was full of luggage. The seats were strewn with blankets and bags. Malarkey picked up a book—*A Perfect Vacuum* by Stanislaw Lem. He dropped it back down. There were shoes under the seats here and there, empty and poignant.

Abdul had made his way to the galley at the back of the plane. Malarkey followed him there.

"Do you want a chicken tikka masala?"

Abdul was standing with a fork and an open aluminium food container. "Not bad for airline food. I think there's some pasta al fredo, if you're interested."

"What are you so cheerful about?

"I'm not cheerful. Just might as well have something to eat, that's all. Have one."

"Stop trying to force feed me. We should go outside and try to find out where we are."

They went back to the cockpit. On their way through the cabin, Malarkey saw that all the seat belts were buckled.

Disembarking was going to be difficult without the usual airport luxury of covered gangways. They decided their best option would be to use the emergency escape chute.

"What's that?"

Abdul was looking out over the wing.

"What?"

"It seems The Welcome Committee is coming out to greet us."

A squad of men was marching towards them over the airfield, rifles on their shoulders, with an officer ahead of them.

"I think they brought us here."

"What? You believe in magic?"

"No, but... actually, yes I do."

"Hmm.... Well, it's definitely very strange."

"Yeah... stranger than life after birth."

Abdul had always had a tendency towards conceptual spoonerisms. Malarkey chuckled.

"You mean after death? Do you think we've died?"

By now the soldiers were twenty yards from the plane, and their officer had called them to a halt. They broke rank and formed a line parallel to the fuselage. They stood at ease, impassive, with their rifle butts resting on the ground.

Except, their rifles were not real guns but sticks.

The men were shirtless and had the word PANAM painted in red letters across their chests. They were barefooted and kilted with cloths wrapped around their waists, secured by belts made of sinews. From the belts hung clusters of shrunken human heads. They stood immobile with ferocious, vacant stares.

"I'd say we're truly fucked, Tariq."

The officer wore an old combat jacket, frayed and unbuttoned, that looked like American issue from the Second World War. On his head was a rusty helmet. He produced a framed photograph and held it out before him like a talisman, facing it towards the aircraft. The whole company stood stock still.

"Not necessarily completely fucked, James. Slightly, perhaps."

Abdul explained the idea that had just come to him. These men outside, as wild as they looked, seemed to have quite an aptitude for military discipline. The obvious thing to do would be to disembark from the plane with an air of overpowering authority and just confirm what they already expected.

"We can be visiting dignitaries. You—Lieutenant Colonel Crusoe, will inspect the troops after I, Sergeant Major Tariq Robinson, have given them a suitable dressing down and licked them into shape."

"You think that will be our ticket to salvation?"

"I don't know. It might be, but what else can we do? We'll have to ham it up, like one of those Monty Python sketches. You know, yell at them and then send them off to the cinema."

It was at moments like these that Malarkey felt a surge of respect for Abdul. The depth of his resilience was unfathomable and sprang from a source of wisdom unbounded by knowledge or doubt.

"You'll have to draw on that colonial superiority, James, that arrogance and racism. You have it in you somewhere. You all do. You have to epitomise disdain and unassailable confidence. Can you do it?"

"I suppose so. Why not? But I should have a swagger stick, or a riding crop."

The men outside remained motionless.

Malarkey went back into the cabin to look for something suitable that a passenger might have left behind, but he couldn't find anything. He would have to go out there without a swagger stick. The thought made him conscious of his arms in an unpleasant way similar to the feeling of insomnia with all its frustration and anxiety. What was he going to do with his hands? It was upsetting to think that his arms would be dangling at his side. Hands and arms were the most crucial symbols of action and intent. To be conscious of their impotence would detract from the impression he needed to make. If he only had some gloves, he could take them off and crush them in one hand, his steely resolve would be apparent—but he did not.

On his way back up front, he looked out of the windows at the strange army that awaited them. Then his eye caught the curved handle of a walking stick like the one his father had used in old age. It was jammed against the wall by a window seat. He pulled it out. There was a rubber tip on the end. This was perfect. He would cut it to length using the saw from the tool kit.

"Look at this, Tariq!"

Malarkey swung the stick under his arm to determine its correct length. "I was just thinking..."

"Impressive."

"Thank you... I was thinking that leaving the plane via the emergency chute is a bad idea. We'll look like a couple of idiots. They'll probably fall over laughing."

This was indeed a problem. Their plan was contingent on making a dignified exit. Malarkey went back to the cockpit to cut the stick..

Abdul was afraid. He gazed at the people outside. The flames were still burning. The effigies had an elemental cruelty. He wondered if they would be stepping off the plane to imminent slaughter, yet the men outside had an air of expectation. They wanted something. There was an opportunity to that.

He looked beyond them. His eyesight was excellent, as was Malarkey's—a prerequisite for pilots. The fog had cleared and he could see that they were in an airport of sorts, a simulacrum of an airport. There were buildings that looked like hangars and a control tower—all made from boughs lashed with vines, their roofs thatched with grasses. Outside one of them was an aircraft, fashioned in a similar way, the skin of its fuselage seemingly made from some kind of rattan. It resembled an American B-29 from the Second World War.

This whole airport was the culmination of prodigious effort and must have taken months, if not years, to construct. It was an image of technology without function, a reinterpretation with the sole purpose of representation. It was a sympathetic magic that had proved most effective—his own unexplained presence here confirmed it.

There was activity in one of the hangars. Six men were struggling with a giant staircase. They were moving it out of the building on rollers made from tree trunks. The two men at the back would take the exposed roller forward and place it under the front of the staircase when the space below it opened up. It was a laborious process, and difficult on the uneven ground. It nearly toppled several times. It was strange they were not using wheels. He looked at the B-29 but it had no wheels either. They had made the landing gear to look like the talons of a giant bird.

There was a seventh man with them who was doing nothing to help. He just walked alongside the others. As he approached, Abdul could see that he appeared to be a radio operator, or was assuming that role. He wore headphones and carried a large rectangular pack on his back, from which emanated a long antenna, made from a sapling.

"I think our problem with the chute has just been solved. They're bringing out a staircase for us."

Malarkey came out of the cockpit with his swagger stick cut to length and joined Abdul at the window. The men outside were pushing the steps into place.

"You know, James, we should probably give them something."

"How many of them are there?"

Abdul counted them through the window.

"Twenty-four, including the officer."

"Let's give them all life jackets," Malarkey was grinning as he turned back into the cabin and began pulling them from beneath the seats and tossing them into the aisle. There was a laptop computer in business class. He checked and saw that the battery was almost fully charged.

"We'll give this to the officer. It should keep him occupied."

They stacked the life jackets by the door and readied themselves. Abdul straightened Malarkey's jacket, patting it down and brushing off some lint with his hands. He still had his eye for style, Malarkey thought. It reminded him of those bygone days, which seemed simpler and more innocent now. They both donned their pilot caps.

"Ready, Tariq?"

The air outside was warm and sultry. Unfortunately the steps were not quite high enough. Malarkey did his best to negotiate the first empty eighteen inches with dignity. His swagger stick was tucked under his left arm and he carried the computer vertically in his right hand, which left no hands free for balance.

When he reached the bottom he went straight to the officer and handed him the laptop. The man had to adjust his grip on the photograph in order to receive it. Malarkey could see that it was a framed, but not glazed, picture of President Eisenhower, or General, as he was at the time. It was barely recognisable, blotched from years of humidity—a disintegrating photograph. Then he took a step backwards and gave a crisp military salute. He was pleased with its effect. The officer was encumbered by the photograph and the computer, and his previously fierce confidence seemed diminished.

"Yupela bin kam long ples balus bilong mipela pinis tru."

Malarkey had no idea what he was talking about. He was saved by Abdul who had followed him down, and who also saluted the officer with deft military precision—the long way up and the short way down. Then he turned to the men and bellowed out:

"Roit then, you 'orrible little bleeders!!!"

The men threw themselves face down on the ground.

Abdul puffed himself up and gave a deafening yell.

"On your feet! Where did you learn soldiering? St Trinian's School for girls? Atten...Shun!"

They seemed to understand and got back on their feet, shuffling half-heartedly into line.

Malarkey walked briskly over to inspect them. The officer had opened the laptop and was pressing the keys with one finger. The photograph of Ike lay on the ground, staring into the sky.

Abdul proceeded to shout at the company before him:

"Salute an officer, you fucking bastards!"

Malarkey watched as a few of them made clumsy attempts. The military salute obviously had little meaning for them. It was really a ridiculous activity.

He passed down the line, pausing momentarily in front of each man, just long enough to stare into his eyes, direct his gaze downwards to his feet and then back up to his eyes again, all the while allowing his face to express a cold disdain. It was more a deliberate lack of expression, or a wilful repression, as if his nostrils were filled with a foul stench and he had the self control to show no sign of it.

He uttered not a word and moved down the line. He was surprised by his own courage. Any one of these men could have killed him with no compunction and probably eaten him and shrunk his head to the size of a tennis ball.

"I think it's time to hand out the life jackets, Sergeant Major."

"Yes sir."

"Have a couple of chaps fetch them."

Malarkey strode off with his stick still under his arm. He saluted the officer again as he passed but only received a menacing stare.

"Mipela nidim kago."

He paused and as the officer closed the computer, he could have sworn that it looked as if he was on the internet, but that was impossible.

"Papa Ike bin promisim givim mipela kago."

He looked around and waved his arm, as if to express his thoughts more clearly.

"Mipela wetim longpela taim. Olgeta bagarap."

Though Malarkey couldn't understand exactly what he was saying, he got the gist of it. He could feel the complaining tone.

This was dangerous. Those in positions of authority were always frightened of being usurped. Malarkey could picture the situation. This man wielded power. He had perhaps maintained it with a promise—that one day an aircraft would come, as long as his subjects obeyed him and followed his instructions, which were quite extensive considering the pseudo airport they had built. He was the sole person among them who understood the mystery. He imbued it with a religious significance and he had no doubt girded it with the tradition of a golden age—perhaps a folk memory of encounters with American GIs—spinning it all into a legend of a god who has departed but will one day return. Did he believe it himself? Malarkey suspected he did not, or not to the same extent as his followers. Cynicism and expedience were the corrosive bedfellows of power. But now their arrival had confirmed his promise and yet at the same time had eclipsed him. He felt threatened and his response might be sudden and irrational.

Malarkey had not slept for over twenty-four hours. He found it difficult to keep up this act of unquestionable superiority. Fear was lurking in the wings. It would be disastrous if he succumbed. He found his way round it by allowing himself to feel genuine dislike. This man was a proto-capitalist and most likely a misogynist too. He had no sense of humour. He took himself too seriously. Where were all the women? There must be some. He would give them the suitcases the stewardesses had left behind.

It was no wonder, he thought, that capitalism had become such a dominant force in economics. It stemmed from the individual desire for survival, second nature for most people, or first perhaps. But it wasn't inevitable or the best possible system, no matter what claims it made for itself. His idea of individuality was mischievous and contradictory and didn't require one person's gain to be another's loss. There was always the sense of wholeness among the separate parts. He attributed it to his Irish forebears, even though they had been the wrong kind of Irish. It was what Abdul referred to as the 'lark' in Malarkey. He would never respect authority, including his own, and he certainly did not respect this man before him.

He turned towards the plane and climbed the steps, half expecting a projectile to hit him between the shoulder blades, but he didn't look back. He stepped past Abdul who was standing in the open doorway demonstrating how to put on and inflate the life jackets. He did not quite have the dexterous choreography of the cabin crew, who did it every day—adept at their charade of safety in an insecure world, but his sign language and stream of invective seemed to be working. They had all put on their jackets and were busy inflating them, some pulling the cords and others blowing the tubes. They were an odd sight with the shrunken heads swinging below the bulky orange jackets—stranger indeed than life after birth. He noticed that Abdul had drawn the curtains to the cabins, obviously to maintain the mystery when the men had come on board to collect the jackets. He had a beautiful attention to detail for things like that.

"Come on Tariq, close the door. We are going to display the modern jet engine at work."

He brushed past the curtain, went forward to the cockpit and climbed into his seat.

Abdul joined him minutes later. He was wondering if he should mention what had happened with the radio operator, but he could see it wasn't the right time. Malarkey had started the engines and was absorbed with the instruments.

The radio operator had seemed anxious, as if it was a matter of great importance.

"Yupela mas harim!"

He had handed him the headphones, which were the two halves of a coconut shell joined by a strip of hide. Abdul, softening his harsh demeanour, had put them on expecting to hear nothing more than the noise from his own head—what he used to think of as the sound of the sea when he cupped his ears as a child, but he heard music instead. It sounded like an ancient Chinese classical orchestra.

***

"Captain James Malarkey here. Air traffic control has informed me that there's a plane ahead of us. We're in a holding pattern at the moment but we should be down in ten or fifteen minutes. It is now thirteen degrees outside and is raining lightly. Thank you for joining us on board today. We look forward to fulfilling your travel needs in the future."

What he was looking forward to was the shower he would take when he got home. It wouldn't be the same now that Klaus wasn't there to greet him with his energetic and uncomplicated love, but it was impossible for a pilot to care for a dog without help.

"What are you doing this weekend, Tariq?"

"Nothing special. I might do a little gardening."

"Do you want to meet me at The Stanhope? They have live jazz on Sundays. It's usually pretty good."

"Maybe."

The Dragon King's Palace

Propelled silently by his frog feet, the diver floated toward his destination. There was no light, except for the murky beam from his waterproof torch. He couldn't be sure he was going the right way. He tried to recall the instructions he had received before setting out. The noise of his breathing filled his ears, along with the muffled, slow motion sounds of the deep.

He was too old for this line of work. He felt his thickening midriff against his wet suit. As dangerous as these missions were, he was more concerned with the normal decline of ageing as a civilian. How long did he have left, if he managed to stay alive today? Five years? Ten? Twenty at most? Twenty years seemed like a day.

His job was not only to set the limpet mines on the doors of The Dragon King's Palace, but to be a redeeming symbol—a figurehead of a nation that yearned for its disintegrated empire. No doubt the Government liked nostalgia as a distraction from the drab existence it provided, and perhaps as a means to generate some cash. Two birds with one stone. If they couldn't have the real thing any more, they could have an image of it..

It wasn't just that he had to be a secret commando, but a public persona too. He was both covert and overt, but if the government wanted to pay him to be a paradox, then at least he would have some fun to make up for the meagre salary they provided. That had always been his philosophy. He was older now.

His name might be Bond. At least it wasn't Tintin. Maybe he could be called something different but similar: Bondla, Benz, Bland. James Bland. Perhaps something even further removed like Binder—Quentin Binder.

His mother, née Valery McGuiness, had dreamed the night before he was born that she should name him Tarquinius. The next day she gave up the idea, obviously not trusting her subconscious, and so Quentin entered the world via his mother and a hospital in East Acton. There had been talk about Tarquinius as a middle name—Quentin Tarquinius. His father, a chain-smoking novelist, regarded by many as a shit, thought it sounded like Ancient Rome. So it became just Quentin, with no middle name. But what was wrong with Ancient Rome, aside from the obvious?

Some years later when he was playing in the garden with some friends, his mother took him aside and told him he would never amount to much. Or was it on a train, in a tunnel, beneath the Alps? What mattered was that it was said, not where the telling took place.

The thought came to him unannounced from the deep. Had she been right or wrong? It seemed so irrelevant now, and he wondered why she had ever bothered saying it.

He shone his dim light on his diver's watch, strapped to his wrist with thick rubber. Where was this Dragon King's Palace? He had no idea what its real name was. He knew what it was supposed to look like though. At the briefing they had shown him blurred photographs—giant gates, large enough to let a submarine pass through, set in reinforced ferrous concrete. An underwater city. Who could build such a monstrosity? A rogue nation? Some dark global conglomerate? Chinese folklore was rife with dragon kings living beneath oceans and rivers. Maybe the Chinese were involved. He was going to breach this place anyway. He should be there by now, according to what they had told him, but he knew they weren't completely trustworthy. He worried that the undercurrents had caused him to drift off course. He might never arrive.

His oxygen supply was diminishing and he was on the point of deciding to surface. He would be a speck on the ocean, waiting for the Royal Navy to retrieve him. He would be almost impossible to see, so he had been equipped with a transmitter to aid in locating him, and an automatically inflatable dinghy strapped in a pouch below the air tank. He wasn't certain they would work. Still, better to take his chances above than below, with its lonely asphyxiation.

That Hermetic axiom—as above, so below is not true when it comes to oceans. The surface is quite different from the bed. They are not remotely similar.

His brain was babbling to itself again. Not a good sign. When he was younger he had always been completely focused on his work, to such an extent that he would feel detached. He had been purely a mechanism let loose on a purpose. That was when he was on a mission. When he had downtime he could carouse and womanise with the best of them. In fact he was the best of them. But now he was detached in a different way by a mind that was not interested in the mission, didn't even know what it was, or couldn't remember. Instead it subjected him to a flow of non-sequiturs that were both attractive and abhorrent. Perhaps it was the rubber tasting air he breathed, or the loneliness.

He had to pay attention and get control of himself, or otherwise he would perish in a swirl of dreams. It was time to go back up, while he still had the chance. He would have to abort the mission. He was not to blame. The information he had been given was incomplete, the equipment provided sub par. It was a classic error of bureaucracy, where details contradicted themselves amongst inter-departmental bickering. Then it occurred to him that maybe their ineptitude was deliberate. They might regard him as an embarrassment, a tool that had outlived its purpose. The dashing arrogance of a handsome youth was not attractive in a man his age. It was ridiculous and counterproductive but they would look like fools if they suddenly abandoned the cause they had championed for so long. It would be much better if their hero was lost at sea, doing his duty until the end. He had the horrible feeling that the Navy would not come looking for him, should he reach the surface. They were letting him go.

As he began to rise upward, he noticed a sudden change in the environment, the equivalent of a dust cloud—churning sand most likely. He felt a distinct, rumbling vibration. He looked down and saw a submarine gliding below him like a giant barracuda. Ahead of it, two gates were sliding open. In an instant his younger self returned and he knew what he had to do without thinking. He immediately swam down and grabbed a rail on the conning tower. His instructions had been only to mine the gates, but now that they were open a bigger prize beckoned.

The submarine entered the chamber and the doors closed behind it. He loosened his grip from the rail and drifted off. This was obviously a kind of lock. The water would be pumped out, and air would be pumped in to allow the craft to moor and the crew to exit. His instructions were to blow the doors, but it would be an added bonus if he blew the pump vents as well.

He needed to remain hidden while the crew disembarked, so he dived down under the starboard side of the submarine—the port side abutted the quay. When it was safe he would mine the doors and the vents. He had five limpets, he might as well put one on the submarine too. As he waited, he opened the satchel that was strapped to his stomach and attached a magnetic mine to the hull. Suddenly the water level started to drop and he was dragged towards the nearest vent. There was nothing for him to hold on to, and he soon found himself pinned against the grate as the water was sucked from the room. He could only hope the level wouldn't drop too far, leaving him exposed. He had set the timer of the limpet on the submarine for two hours. That should give him enough time to mine the doors and vents, and to make his exit. He would have to find another way out.

The pumps stopped. Seconds later the room burst into light—sodium vapour lights. He could see them from beneath the water. He was luckily still submerged but not deep enough to avoid discovery. He had a few seconds before the crew left the vessel and any maintenance people came to greet them. He swam back to his hiding place beneath the hull and waited. He heard the hatch opening. After giving himself thirty minutes rest, he swam over to the doors and attached the mines, setting the timers for one and a half hours. Then he placed the remainder on two of the pump vents, with the same time delay. Lastly he removed the empty satchel and secured it to the grille on one of the vents. It was a precaution in case he was apprehended, and might prevent his sabotage from being noticed, or at least delay its discovery. The time had come to enter the Dragon King's Palace.

He let his head break the surface of the water. He was in a large, cavernous room. An arched ceiling stretched over him.

The walls were hospital green. There were five other quays, one of which was occupied by the submarine, the rest empty. He did not detect any sign of people. He swam over to an empty dock and climbed the steps, pausing to take off his flippers. He removed his Beretta from its waterproof container and attached the silencer, then he turned off the air cylinder, leaving it strapped to his back. It was cumbersome but he only had an hour to make his exit, and didn't want to lose time retrieving it.

Aside from the sea gates he had mined, there was only one other door leading out of the dock area. It was marked with a symbol, or group of symbols, that reminded him of cuneiform. It had a wheel lock, as on the door to a bank vault. He stood before it and listened. No sound. He glanced at his watch. Eighty-five minutes left.

He put his hands to the wheel, and with the sensitivity of a cat burglar began to turn it. Instantly the silence was rent by the shrieking of klaxons. More lights came on and began flashing with a frequency he feared would resonate with his brain.

The door swung open and twelve men poured through, each one armed with a submachine gun. He evaluated his options and decided that the best was surrender, which he did immediately. His captors disarmed him and ushered him into the sunken city.

They were all young and lithe, and were dressed alike—black trousers, combat boots, black shirts with the same cuneiform symbols that were on the door, monogrammed on the left side of each chest in white. There was not an ounce of flab among them. Chiseled jaws and close cropped hair. They looked like fashion models. These were not the soldiers of an army, but the accoutrements of an autocrat. The attention to appearance and aesthetics suggested a single mind, not a committee. They were no doubt taking him to an audience with the Dragon King.

They led him down several long corridors. This place was big. They stopped at a door with a porthole. He tried to look through it but was blocked by his guards. They paused long enough to open a recessed cabinet in the wall and take out hairnets for each of them, including himself, even though his head was encased in rubber. Then they took him inside. The walls were filled with banks of slowly spinning wheels, stopping and starting, going in one direction and then the reverse, spooling tape between them. This room must be a computer. At the far end was a low console desk, forming a gentle arc. At its centre was a high backed chair. After a few studied seconds it swivelled to face them.

The Dragon King was a woman.

"We've been expecting you Mr Binder." She smiled, "well, not really, but we have been following your exploits."

"I hope you have been suitably entertained."

"Entertained... Yes. Very amusing," she frowned. "Don't they have a place for people like you, Mr Binder, who have outlived their usefulness?"

"They do. But I'm not at liberty to talk about it."

She looked him over and raised her eyebrows.

"You look a little past your prime for this sort of thing, Mr Binder."

"I do it for pleasure. There's no age limit to that."

Despite his waning libido, he could imagine an intimate evening. A game of cat and mouse, some drinks.

"I'm curious as to whom we owe the honour of your visit, Mr Binder."

"I was just passing by and I thought I'd stop in. I've heard so much about you."

She turned her attention to the guards.

"Get him out of this ridiculous diving suit and give him some clothes."

Then she turned back to him.

"We will continue very soon, Mr Binder, and we will discover why you are here. We have some instruments to help us solve the mystery. You might be interested in seeing them."

On cue, one of the guards stepped forward with a metal briefcase and opened it in front of him. It contained a thumbscrew, a hypodermic syringe and some electrodes with wires attached.

Then he was hustled out of the room and taken to a cell off one of the corridors. On his way he observed as many details of his surroundings as he could, while counting the number of paces he took. When they reached their destination they made him strip naked. It was an awkward process peeling off the rubber suit and the guards were grinning. They searched him and made him wait while one of them went to get him clothes. These turned out to be the same as what they were wearing, down to the monogrammed shirt, though they didn't provide him with footwear. The trousers were too tight and he had to leave the waist button undone, which caused another burst of snickering. Then they left, taking everything with them including his watch. The door clicked shut and he heard the lock engage.

He estimated that there were about fifty minutes left before detonation. He could not know how much damage the explosions would do to the structure as a whole but the pressure at this depth would no doubt exploit any breach. He assumed that he would die within the hour. It seemed rather anticlimactic considering the life he had led.

There was no light in his cell and no furniture. He sat on the floor in the pitch dark. The impossibility of action and the darkness accentuated his thoughts. He had no inkling what was going on here beyond the usual games of power, and MI6 had given him even less information about this mission than usual. He wanted to know the meaning of the cuneiform, it took on an irrational significance. He was convinced that if he understood that, he would somehow be in a better position.

Ancient scripts had always fascinated him as a child—hieroglyphs, cuneiform, Canaanite, Phoenician, early Greek. He had just started to study ancient languages at university when his education had been interrupted by the war and he had been drafted into the army.

If events had unfolded differently, he would be a university professor, publishing books and papers, an erudite mentor to his students. They would be a source of inspiration to each other as they delved into the pleasures of knowledge. But each path taken erases the others around it. There is no return.

The army had quickly led him to the commandos because of his daring nature and physical stamina. From there he had volunteered to join the newly formed and unorthodox secret unit that became known as the SAS. He had felt at home with the relaxed attitude to military tradition and discipline. There he had learned the skills he still used—of sabotage and subterfuge, of audaciousness and the capacity to never be deterred by insurmountable odds.

After the war he had been recruited to the position he held today, no doubt because of his covert experience and his good looks. He had jumped at the opportunity but it had caused his desire for intellectual pursuits to atrophy and wither.

He heard footsteps coming down the corridor—one man. He felt an opportunity presenting itself. Just one man this time. Foolish.

He took up a position flat against the wall by the door, on the opposite side to the hinges. As the door swung open, he gently placed his right hand on top of the man's head and his left on the jaw. In the split second it took for the guard's eyes to adjust between light and dark, he had broken his neck with a quick wrench. The guard was dead at his feet. It was easy. He knew that it was a most selfish act to kill a living being but he felt no remorse. Once you've done it a few times it loses meaning. He dragged the body into the cell, removed the boots and put them on himself. They weren't a bad fit. He took the machine gun and quickly searched for extra ammunition. Finding none, he left the room and locked the door behind him.

Sitting in the dark had interfered with his sense of time. He wasn't certain when the bombs would explode but he estimated that he had about twenty minutes. He needed to escape. Without his diving suit and aqualung his chances of survival were negligible, but he still had twenty minutes and might as well make use of them.

He headed in the opposite direction to the computer room. He passed numerous doors, each marked with the curious cuneiform script but one caught his eye because it also bore the image of a staircase. He opened it. Stairs led up for as far as he could see, and beyond.

He noticed that every ninety-three steps there was a landing. He realised after passing two of them, that they served as decompression zones for a climber rising to the surface.

Ninety-three steps were about sixty feet. He rested a while on each landing. The mines should detonate at any moment. He still expected to be a victim of his own sabotage but at least he would die free, and in the interim he did not want to suffer from the bends. So far he had heard no sign of pursuit, which was odd. He kept the machine gun ready to fire a burst if necessary.

He discovered that there was a cupboard in the wall on every landing with a push release door panel. Inside were water bottles and what looked like military food ration packs. This was a well designed operation. The outside of each door panel was covered with cuneiform script. Who were these people, the New Assyrians? He helped himself to food and water and kept going.

The bombs should have gone off by now. Something must have gone wrong. Even at this distance he was sure he would feel their effect. He couldn't have climbed beyond their reach. His calves were burning. The pain was probably exacerbated by the gas bubbles in his blood, though he had been ascending correctly as far as he could tell. He was desperately tired but could not allow himself to fall asleep. There would be a time for that, maybe, but not yet.

The higher he climbed, the stranger he felt. He could not recall when he had left London, or how long he had been on this mission. He could no longer understand points of reference, which were what he needed to make sense of things. He was exhausted, under stress and had a surfeit of nitrogen in his blood stream. That would be an explanation. Even as a younger man he would have felt these effects, and now he was... how old was he? He couldn't place it. Definitely over fifty, maybe older.

He kept climbing. He imagined that he must have been climbing for almost twenty-four hours. This was the longest staircase he had ever ascended. It beggared the conceivable. The top was nowhere in sight, but the width of the passage seemed to be narrowing. Another landing. No cupboard, no cuneiform. Then bang. He walked into a wall. A dead end.

He collapsed on the floor in crushed defeat. Even for a man of his resilience this was too much. It was cruelty on an existential level, much worse than the suitcase of torture implements the Dragon Queen had wanted him to see. It negated everything. The kind of sadistic joke that only a god could play.

He lay prone in debilitating depression, face down on the floor. The machine gun was pressing into his chest, causing him pain. Eventually he could bear it no longer and got up.

He went over to the offending wall and ran his hands over it. A crack. It was not just a wall, there was a door in it, finely fitted with no handle or hardware, on this side at least. He pushed. The door moved. With his fingertips he wrenched it wide open. Relief flooded through him, invigorating him with energy.

It was dark on the other side and very cold. Something greasy brushed against his shoulder. There were animal carcasses hanging on hooks. He must be in a meat refrigerator. He crossed the room and exited the other side. Again, darkness. He looked around and surmised that this was a butcher's shop. It was obviously night and after business hours. The entrance door had a window in it and he looked out. Beyond the parking area he could see a road and low buildings on the other side. He had surfaced in a small town.

He had to find somewhere to sleep. Not here where the employees would find him when they came to work in the morning, and seeing as the entrance to the deep was in this establishment, that might mean the butcher was affiliated with the Dragon Queen, and he needed to keep away from this place.

He was hungry and made himself a sandwich with some sliced meat he found in a refrigerated cabinet.

He was on the point of leaving when he realised it wouldn't be a good idea to walk down the street in a small town carrying a machine gun. He went back through the meat cellar and propped the gun against the wall on the stairwell side of the door, then closed it. This side had a door knob. As an after thought, he took a rag from the counter and wiped down any surface he could remember touching. Then he unlocked the door to the shop and stepped outside, wiping the handles as he left.

The night was clear and moonlit. He could hear cicadas and it was not cold. It felt like late summer or early autumn. He could have sworn it had been winter when he set out, but there was no point in trying to understand—better summer than winter anyway. The question was, should he turn left or right? It was not an easy decision because both choices seemed equally unimportant. It was quite something to be stymied by unimportance and it gave him pause but he knew he should keep moving. He didn't want to get stopped by the police, who were the only people likely to be around at this time. He passed by two parked cars. They looked like American vehicles. Could he be in America?

A little further up the street he came across a small green—an area of lawn with a flagpole at its centre. He looked up, and though there was no wind and the flag hung limply, he could see that he was indeed in America. He didn't even try to make sense of it.

At the green there was another road to the right and he turned on to it. This decision was easy. It looked like a less populated street. He soon came across a graveyard with a wooded area beyond it. He could find a good place to sleep in the woods, somewhere he wouldn't be disturbed. It was warm enough to sleep outside relatively comfortably.

The next day he awoke with the dawn, badly bitten by mosquitoes and feeling groggy. He would go back into the town and look around, and perhaps find something to eat. He thought he might try to contact Larry Adams, his colleague in the CIA. They had met in Iran when they were both involved in the Mosaddegh operation and had become friends. Though whether friendship was possible between spies was a moot point. He realised that he really didn't have any friends, just acquaintances. That might not be particular to him but a general aspect of ageing. Young people were involved in each other's lives more intensely than their seniors, who tended to drift away with responsibilities—marriages, offspring and the assumed concerns of adulthood. He had none of those responsibilities, yet he still had no friends. So why go back? He decided not to call Larry. It was a stupid idea. He would begin life as a beggar, and see where it led.

It was still early and most of the shops had not yet opened. He hobbled around on aching legs, getting a sense of the place. Though initially it had looked like just one street, he discovered many small side roads and enclaves. It was a bigger town than he had thought. He went back to take a look at the butcher's shop in the daylight. It was open and there were several cars outside. It looked completely normal, nothing that would suggest a deeper significance. He wasn't going to enter it though.

He turned back towards the town centre. He had passed a café on his way down, which seemed like a good prospect. That would be a good starting place. It was not difficult to assume the role of a beggar. Such people had nowhere particular to go, nothing particular to do and nothing to do it with—a condition which described his own situation.

He peered through the window at the customers being served their breakfasts and felt a pang of hunger. Those rations he had found in the stairwell had been adequate but not satisfying. He loitered in front of the building. There was something so simple about having basic needs and he felt more directly connected to humanity than he had in a long time. It seemed ironic that he had to sink so low to climb so high.

A woman stepped passed him. She appraised him quickly and understood.

"Are you hungry? Would you like a muffin and a cup of coffee?

"Please... yes."

"Milk and sugar in your coffee?"

"Just milk, please."

"Hold on."

She came back out and handed him a hot paper cup and a small bag. "There you go."

"Thank you."

Her eyes flitted across the emblazoned cuneiform on his chest."

"I haven't seen you around before. Did you come up from the city?"

"I came up from the bottom of the sea."

He could read the emotions on her face—compassion, curiosity, doubt and amusement, even a hint of fear. She took him for a madman.

"What were you doing down there?"

"Working."

"What kind of work do you do?"

"I'm a secret agent."

She cinched her bag up on her shoulder. "There's a place up there," she indicated the road with the graveyard, "a humanitarian organisation. They might be able to help you with food and somewhere to stay. You should check it out. Number forty-seven I think. What's your name?"

"Wellington. George Wellington."

"Well take care, George."

Reversal

It began when a twelve year-old girl in America started speaking backwards. The first incident occurred when she was at school. The teacher, a Mrs Pendleton, asked her to list the three branches of the United States government. She responded, "Judicial, Executive, Legislative."

There was nothing wrong with her answer, except that she presented the terms in a different order than usual. This was not noticed at the time. The clock on the classroom wall indicated 11:32 am.

Only months later when medical researchers, civil servants and journalists pored over the relevant data, was it deemed consequential. By then it was too late.

Quite possibly it was already too late by 11:33. Since that moment the girl whose name was Jane Watson, soon to be known as Watson Jane, spoke only backwards and she did it as fluently as most people speak forwards.

At first the teachers thought it was a joke. She was an intelligent girl with a subtle sense of humour. She was a good student, attentive and diligent and well liked. But when she persisted they recognised it as a problem and she was sent to the school psychologist.

"Have a seat, Jane. How are you finding school these days?"

"Fine it's."

"You have siblings, don't you?"

"Me than older he's. Brother a and sister little a, yes."

"What do you want to be when you grow up?"

"Man white rich a."

The conversation continued in this way and the psychologist, Dr Alison Frobisher, was at a loss. She had never seen anything like it. Aside from her unusual way of talking, Jane seemed like a normal, happy and healthy child. Her record at school was good, her grades were excellent and she had never had problems with her teachers or classmates.

She noticed that there was a small time lag before Jane responded, which increased proportionally with the length of her questions. This was likely the time it took for translation, which implied that she was not only talking backwards but thinking in reverse too.

This was obviously a serious issue, beyond what she normally dealt with at the school, and she recommended that Jane be examined by a specialist.

Later that evening, Dr Frobisher herself was talking backwards and by the following afternoon her children and husband were doing the same. After that the condition spread like wildfire.

Soon there were media reports and emergency meetings at The Department of Health. By this time it was estimated that seven thousand people were affected and the number was increasing exponentially.

The condition was thought to be caused by a new virus that affected the brain, though it did not seem to cause any other symptoms. Some linguists pointed out that that this kind of speech was not technically reversed, as the phonemes were running in their normal direction and only the word order was affected. If phonemes were spoken backwards, words would begin in a drawn out fashion and end abruptly. This was correct but had no bearing on the gravity of the situation.

No virus was identified and brain imaging of affected people showed no abnormalities. Meanwhile the number of infections had increased to include almost a third of the population.

Opinion as to the cause of this problem varied. There were those who still believed it was due to a virus. Something that could not be found did not preclude its existence. As most diseases in humans have crossed over from another species of animal, they were looking for a vector and suspected it to be Sciurus Carolinensis, the American grey squirrel. Watson Jane was known to have associated with squirrels, feeding them in her back garden.

Others leant towards a bacterial infection. There were people who suspected it was due to an environmental issue such as contamination of the brain with micro plastics. Still others believed the problem to be cultural—an incidence of mass psychosis, and there were those who saw it as a biological weapon used by some malign foreign agent. Some people believed it was divine retribution. Conspiracy theories abounded, involving the mafia, pederasty, aliens and the magnetic field.

There was an increase in traffic accidents due, it was thought, to the misreading of signs. Was the number thirty-five in fact fifty-three?

The rest of the world watched this event unfold with uneasy trepidation, horror and indifference.

The Hierophant

The hierophant, an anonymous mystagogue, sat huddled in an armchair that was not an armchair and looked at the fireplace. All the other furniture in the room had been broken up and fed to the flames which were the only source of light.

There were also four young men in the room. They were the ones who had smashed up the furniture for firewood.

The Hierophant was an old man and when he spoke his voice was very high. Why he happened to be there no one knew.

The youths were there because they needed somewhere to live. They were all going to become rich one day but at that moment they were very poor and had next to nothing between them. They shared what little they had. Paying rent was out of the question, not that any landlord would have wished to accommodate them, the way they carried on.

One among them, whom we shall henceforth refer to as Youth Number Three, had a knack for befriending wealthy women. Whenever they took off to summer on the island of Mustique, or some other exotic place they would let him stay in their houses. Once settled, Three would invite the others to join him. The houses were always in the most exclusive areas and were clean and exquisitely decorated. They would all enjoy a few months of luxury, then move on to somewhere else. Whether Three had to pimp himself out was his own business .

In one of these houses Youth Number Two came across a VCR. He had never seen one before. It was the stuff of science fiction, and gave him the same intense pleasure as when he had first tasted an avocado. He pushed a video cassette into the slot and sat back in a comfortable chair with his feet upon an ottoman. He watched *Lacombe Lucien* by Louis Malle, a film about an uncouth French country boy who unwittingly at first, collaborates with the Nazis, then goes on to betray them. A study of amorality. It completely absorbed him. The room was filled with a gentle greenish light.

The house where they now sat in the dark was not that kind of place. It was in the process of being sold and had the empty feeling of life that had moved elsewhere, leaving unintelligible memories behind. There was no electricity and no heat. It had obviously once been a fine house, and was full of unusual architectural details.

The boys sat around with the Hierophant, who silently gazed at the flames. They offered him hashish and bottles of beer. It was like having a campfire indoors. He smiled and said little. At one point he suddenly giggled and commented that Youth Four was an androsphinx. They had no idea what he meant but hung on his words. He not only had a very high pitched voice but he spoke so softly that he was barely audible.

The Hierophant didn't elaborate on his androsphinx comment and the boys bantered amongst themselves. Despite their bravado, each one of them was waiting for him to offer them the fruit of his wisdom—to describe the experiences of his past in a way that would direct their lives in the present and lead them on a path through illusive reality. It was not so many years since they had been at school, and they still thought in terms of being taught.

This is not something they would have admitted to themselves or each other, had they been aware of it. It is only the way these words are arranged that makes such a meaning possible.

Youth Three and Four were fencing on the stairs. Three always travelled with a couple of foils. They all had something—Youth Two had a scroll. The night wore on.

The Hierophant spoke little because he had nothing to say. "What is a thought?" he thought. He watched the twisting flames. They were better than television. He had no inkling why he was there but he didn't mind. He enjoyed the company of these boys. He liked their brash energy and their humour, their eager sincerity and their insouciance, their slim bodies and their naïveté, their closeness.

The fire dwindled to glowing embers. There was no furniture left to burn. The coldness and damp closed in around them with a lupine tenacity and cunning. It was time to sleep.

Youth Two was the first to leave the circle. He had a feeling of disquiet, a sneaking suspicion that everything might be nothing. His mood lifted when he found a room with a bed in it. There was even a blanket. He wouldn't have to sleep on the floor. He was lucky. He kicked off his shoes.

When he awoke the room was full of light, softly corrupted by the grimy window panes. He could take in his surroundings. He was pleasantly surprised. It was a comfortable room, perfectly sized. The walls were a yellowing, flakey white. The peeling paint suggested maps of non-existent places. The oddest thing about it were the two sets of double doors which faced him as he lay on the bed, and which he hadn't noticed the night before.

There was an entrance from the hallway, then four feet of empty space and beyond that a wall with interior windows and another set of double doors, also with windows in the upper halves, all painted in ancient, creamy white.

He got up and went down into the street. The others must have still been asleep. He was hungry but only had enough for some cigarettes and the Sunday paper.

When he got back he lay on the bed and took out the magazine that was always included on Sundays. He skimmed through it and found an article that looked interesting. It was about a famous man who had killed himself ten years earlier by taking a drug overdose. It suggested that new information and some unanswered questions threw the verdict of suicide into doubt.

The man had two servants who lived with him, a husband and wife. He told the wife that he was going to rest in his room. At least twelve hours passed and he didn't emerge, then in the middle of the night she received a phone call from someone who did not identify himself. He asked how her employer was, referring to him by his first name. He'd heard there had been an accident. Then he hung up.

Feeling worried, she went upstairs to check. She opened the doors from the hall and then knocked on the interior doors. She looked through the glass, and though the room was dark she could see that he was in bed. On receiving no response, she entered and found that he was dead.

The article speculated that he had been poisoned, perhaps because he had run foul of organised crime in New York. He was a small time businessman whose experience had not grown as fast as his business and he was out of his depth. The maid said that apart from the anonymous phone call, no one else had contacted him or come to the house in Chapel Street that day.

Two let the magazine fall on his knees. This building was in Chapel Street. Though the article didn't mention the address, the maid's description of the double doors and the interior windows was just too uncanny.

He was in the room he was reading about. He was certain of it, and suspected that he was even lying in the same bed. It might be a coincidence, he supposed, some strange manifestation of chance. But then chance was not what it seemed to be. It was deeply disturbing—a horrible recursion. He could not remain in the room.

He sprang off the bed, the magazine in his hand, and went to look for the others. When he told them what had happened and showed them the article they didn't seem particularly concerned or interested. He couldn't understand it. How could anyone not see the importance of this? Or could it be that it just pertained to him, as he had been the only one in the room? Perhaps the haunted one played a part in his own haunting. He wasn't sure what it meant but this twisting of reality must have some significance.

His friends suddenly appeared two dimensional to him, distant and shallow like strangers. He would go and tell the Hierophant.

But the Hierophant was nowhere to be found.

The Bohemian Adventure

I have endeavoured to present the public with accounts of my friend, Sherlock Holmes, and of his singular intelligence, his vigour and his courage. He often joked with me that his great fame was due solely to my embellishments. He would have preferred to lead a quiet existence, engaged with his chemical experiments, and would no doubt have done so were it not for the exigencies of crime and his need for the stimulus of unsolved questions.

I have had the honour to accompany him on many of his adventures and must confess that I always leapt at these opportunities, often I fear to the detriment of my wife and of my medical practice.

It is with hesitation that I now take up my pen. The sensitivity of some of our adventures has necessitated their omission from my records on account of their connection to Government affairs, or to the Royal Houses of Europe. The occasion upon which I now write was not among that variety. My hesitation is due to the catastrophic effect this case had on my old friend. However, it was so singular and unlike any that had come before that I believe it must be recorded.

It began innocently enough. It was a day towards the end of February in '06. My practice had been quiet and my wife was away on a visit to friends. The cold and damp of the season were bothering my old Afghani wound, as was often the case at that time of year. The pain and the inclement weather caused me to feel melancholy, so I decided to call on my old friend. It had been some time since we had last met.

I took a hansom cab and when I arrived at Baker Street found Holmes engaged with his violin. He threw it down upon the sofa as I entered. The intimacy between two gentlemen who had lodged together left me well acquainted with his eccentricities but his nonchalance with the instrument surprised me nonetheless. He was fastidious in his affairs but had a carefree attitude towards his possessions. In the days when we had lived together I would often find his pipe tobacco in a slipper and his garments strewn haphazardly over the furniture.

"Watson, what luck!"

There was a gleam in his eye and an energy across his features that presaged a new adventure. He pulled a chair close to the hearth.

"Sit here by the fire. It will relieve your pain. I shall ask Mrs Hudson to bring us up some tea."

He had no doubt noticed that my shoes were clean and that I had therefore arrived by cab and knowing my preference for walking, had deduced that my wound was bothering me. This did not impress me as it might once have done. I had become accustomed to his habits, though I never ceased to appreciate his extensive and rapid observation of detail.

"Do you have a new case?"

"We are expecting a visitor, a Mrs Violet Saunders. She wrote to me by morning post requesting a consultation. It has been a fallow period, Watson. I think perhaps I have been too successful in my work."

I was glad to see Holmes in such high spirits and it elevated my own mood. Mrs. Hudson served us tea and afterwards we sat back with cigars.

"Do you have any particulars of this case that you might share with me?"

"Nothing at all," said he as he sprang from his chair and leapt to the window. "I believe our guest is arriving now. She has a fine pair of horses."

I rose to join him at the window. The horses were fine indeed, as was the carriage. This was a lady of substance.

Moments later we heard her on the stair outside the door and then she entered. She was a presence that commanded attention. I estimated her age to be in the middle thirties. She was a figure of exquisite beauty and intelligence, but these were not the only qualities that drew me to her. She had another quality, which try as I might I was unable to determine.

Holmes summoned the charm that came so easily to him, "My dear Mrs Saunders, please be seated."

During the many years we had been acquainted, Holmes had never shown any remote interest in women. I imagine he considered them ruled by emotion, a state so antithetical to his own nature. However his lack of interest had in no way diminished his gallant manner when communicating with the female sex. He offered her the chair I had just vacated.

Mrs Saunders settled herself by the fire and Holmes perched on the arm of a chair opposite her. I stood next to the table, allowing myself to rest against it and take the weight off my painful leg.

"This is my colleague and biographer, Dr Watson. You may be as candid with him as you would be with me. Before we proceed, may I offer you tea?"

"No thank you, Mr Holmes, though I would very much like a cigar."

This was an unusual request but Holmes, without a trace of emotion and with his customary energetic grace, produced the box and lit her cigar, striking a match against his shoe.

"Pray tell us what has brought you here."

Mrs Saunders drew on her cigar before answering. "There have been some strange occurrences at my house." She sat back again with her incongruous cigar.

"The details if you please," said Holmes with a hint of impatience.

"There have been frequent break-ins."

"And what may I ask has been stolen from you?"

"Nothing at all."

"Where might you reside?"

"Cavendish Square, number sixty-eight. Nothing has been taken, Mr Holmes, quite the reverse, things have been added."

Most clients arrived in a state of nervous exhaustion or indecision and helplessness but Mrs Saunders seemed very much at ease. She was in no hurry to state her business, something I knew would vex Holmes, though he repressed any expression of annoyance.

"What are these things that have appeared in your house?"

Mrs Saunders leaned back in her chair in a rather uncouth manner. Her graceful neck was adorned with a string of delicate pearls. Her dress was cut scandalously low, even for the fashion of our modern times.

"The first thing to arrive, Mr Holmes, was a flute. Farrel discovered it on the davenport, beneath some papers."

"Who is this Farrel?"

"He is my butler."

"And there have been other appearances?"

"Yes, almost every day something else shows up. After the flute there was an oil painting lying flat on the carpet in the drawing room. I believe it to be that famous painting The Duchess of Devonshire."

"Are you certain it was that painting? It was stolen, you know, from Mr Agnew some thirty years past and I believe it is now in America. Is it still in your possession?"

"It is not, and I cannot be sure whether it was the original painting or merely a copy. I am not well versed in these matters. You see, Mr Holmes, the items that appear in my house disappear soon after."

"How many servants are in your employ, Mrs Saunders?"

"Six. A butler, three maids, a coachman and a cook."

"They all reside with you?"

"All but the coachman."

"Does your husband have an opinion on the matter?"

"Alas, I am a widow and I live alone."

"What other items have mysteriously appeared and vanished?"

"A spinning wheel, a child's doll, a stack of leather-bound books concerning occult esoterica, and a terracotta urn in Grecian style. I think that is the sum."

"When did these appearances start to occur?"

"On the night of February 14th. I remember clearly because on that evening I attended a gathering of friends. I stayed out late and it was upon my waking the next day that Farrel discovered the flute."

"Where did this gathering take place?"

"I do not consider that to be relevant, Mr Holmes."

This was the first time I noticed a tension growing between them.

"One of the first lessons in the business of detection, Madam, is that no detail is irrelevant no matter how insignificant it may appear until proven otherwise. The address if you please."

"One hundred and forty-three Cleveland Street."

"The occasion of the gathering?"

Mrs Saunders fingered her cigar, avoiding his keen gaze for a second or two.

"It is the studio and residence of an artist friend, who hosts a salon there from time to time."

"Thank you. I take it you have informed the police about these occurrences?"

"I have not. I decided to approach you first, Mr Holmes. Your reputation is widespread and impeccable. Any fee you may require is no hindrance."

I could tell that Holmes had garnered all he wanted from this woman but she showed no inclination to leave. He rose and went to the window, seeing as I did myself that the fine carriage was still waiting in the street below. The horses were muzzled with nosebags.

"Thank you Mrs Saunders. This concludes our interview at present. I now have other matters to attend to, but I shall look into your case and hope to provide you with an answer in a few days' time."

After our visitor had left, Holmes poured two tumblers of brandy and we sat in front of the fire, I resumed my original place. We spent a few minutes in silence as Holmes packed his pipe and I watched the dancing flames.

"What do you make of it, Watson?

I had not yet formed an opinion. The whole affair made no sense to me. I felt that he was testing my powers of observation and inference when he asked this question, which he invariably did whenever I was witness to one of these interviews. He was always far ahead of me and knew it.

"What perplexes me Holmes, assuming her account to be truthful, is what possible object a man might have that would lead him to deposit random items in someone else's house. Theft I could understand. It is of course illegal to enter a residence surreptitiously and without invitation but beyond that I cannot see what crime has taken place here."

"What makes you assume there was an illegal entry? These acts may just as well have been committed by a person already on the inside, or they may not have been committed at all. Items that appear then vanish may never have appeared in the first place, so then there would be no entry, illegal or otherwise."

"Do you have a solution?"

"I must first acquire information and arrange the facts. Tomorrow I shall go to Cavendish Square and make an examination of the premises. I believe this case may well be more profound than we had initially supposed."

We relaxed back again to silence, enjoying the warmth of the fire. I was thinking through the affair and trying to apply my friend's methods.

"Another thing that strikes me Holmes, is that she did not report this matter to the police. One would expect that they would be the first recourse for most people in such a circumstance. That lends doubt to her veracity. My intuition tells me she is not completely to be trusted."

"Excellent, Watson. It amuses me to wonder what the police would make of it. As we well know, Scotland Yard has the ability to gather facts but not to comprehend them. However, your reliance on intuition disappoints me. It is not worth much unless supported by facts, and when that is the case it is no longer intuition. Do you recall her reticence about providing the address in Cleveland Street?"

I nodded.

"That street is the very heart of Bohemia, a place where the normal divisions of society do not apply. Aristocrats mingle with ladies of the night, artists, anarchists, gypsies and so forth. Our Mrs Saunders is a Bohemian. One thing is certain, she is not who she would have us believe her to be. A woman with a coachman and a carriage of that quality and a fine pair to draw it would not depart with a half-smoked cigar, even if such a person should smoke cigars. She would have left it in the ashtray. Did you not notice that?"

I went home in an unsettled mood without knowing the cause. In hindsight I see it as a sense of foreboding about those events surrounding my friend, an emotion he would have vehemently decried.

The following day I resumed the duties of my practice. I was glad to find that the condition of my wound had ameliorated. I discussed the case with my wife, now returned. She held the same opinion as me, that Mrs Saunders was not to be trusted. One aspect of our conjugal harmony was our enjoyment of discussing these cases.

As always, when embarked on a venture with Holmes, I was filled with excitement and impatient curiosity. The hours of the day passed slowly but as soon as I was able I returned to Baker Street. Holmes was not there when I arrived so I smoked several cigarettes and tried to amuse myself with a novel.

I had not long to wait before Holmes burst into the room with the energy of a hound on the chase.

"It is just as I thought, Watson. Mrs Saunders does not exist, and there never has been a Mr Saunders."

"Pray elaborate."

He took off his coat and threw it across the sofa, then reached for his box of cigarettes.

"The property at the address she gave us in Cavendish Square belongs to a gentleman named Sir Robert Foote. He was present and was kind enough to invite me in. There have been no strange events at the house and neither he, nor his wife, nor their servants have ever seen or heard of our beautiful Bohemian. What do you think of that?"

"It only confirms my intuition. Mrs Saunders, whoever she may be, is not trustworthy. The whole thing was probably a prank, an unfortunate consequence of your fame perhaps."

"It is more than that, Watson. Much more, and it does not bode well."

I did not understand the gravity he attached to this situation.

"What is your concern, Holmes?"

"Someone is attempting to manipulate me. It is like one of those card tricks. The conjurer invites you to pick a card. With some sleight of hand he determines the card you have picked. He stacks the cards into piles and asks you to select one. Knowing its location he leaves the pile on the table if it contains your card and removes it if it does not. The process continues until there is one pile left, which is then subdivided into individual cards. The game goes on until only one card remains. The conjurer turns it over. It is the card you have chosen. You are amazed but the conjurer has known the outcome all along. He has guided your choices. The decisions you thought you had made were in fact his own. Something like that is going on here, Watson, but I am fully aware of it and not credulous."

"What will be your course of action?"

"It will be to visit the address she gave us in Cleveland Street. If she was truthful on that account, which I believe she was, it will confirm my suspicion that someone of equal intelligence to mine intends me to go to Cleveland Street, and go there I shall, but forewarned."

The case was fast exceeding my expectations.

"Do you foresee danger?"

"I do, which is why I ask that you accompany me, should you be willing."

"Of course."

"You should make sure you bring your revolver with you, Watson. However, before we make this excursion I shall have my street Arabs reconnoitre for us."

Holmes made use of this gang of urchins on occasion. They were the perfect choice for intelligence gathering, able to move unobserved and unsuspected. Their youthful alacrity and hunger for coins, with I imagine a little coaching from Holmes, made them very effective spies. The information they provided was of benefit more often than not.

"But what is the object in luring you to Cleveland Street?"

"I do not yet know, Watson, but it is no doubt malign. Mrs Saunders is a professional actress and a good one. The carriage in which she arrived tells us that there are considerable funds behind this venture and that only makes the situation graver."

"Why would she give you an obviously false address in Cavendish Square? Anybody would know that you would see through such a simple ruse. What is to be gained by that?"

"Everything she did from the moment she arrived, and even before, was done by design. Her request for a cigar was to throw us off guard. The account of the appearances and disappearances was calculated to titillate the imagination with an inherent absurdity that could be interpreted as a mystery. Even that distinction had a purpose. The mention of the famous Gainsborough painting, an improbability, since that after its rediscovery by the Pinkertons it was gobbled up at auction and returned to America, was introduced to sow doubt."

"Why should she wish us to doubt her story?"

"Because, my dear Watson, the manipulator must control doubt just as much as credulity if he is to have the greatest effect upon his victim but pray allow me to continue. The address in Cavendish Square, so easily proved false, was intended to show me that I was being manipulated and that I was not the one with the upper hand. I was foolish enough to fall for her reticence about revealing the address in Cleveland Street. Her intention was to rouse my curiosity and nudge me towards where they want me to go."

"This is madness, Holmes. If you are being manipulated as you say, then why would you go where they want you to?"

"Someone is at my game, Watson, and with a singular skill. There is beauty in a contest between equals."

"You are well known and respected for solving perplexing questions but does this even constitute a case? As far as I can tell, no crime has been committed."

"Not yet, Watson. Not yet."

There was a rustle at the door and a boy stood before us, barefooted and grimy with London soot. This was Tom, the leader of the urchins Holmes employed. I had met him before.

On previous occasions the whole gang would show up when summoned but this had so distressed Mrs Hudson that Tom now came alone. He would disseminate the instructions he received, along with the pay, to his young colleagues somewhere far from Baker Street.

Holmes explained what was required and included a very detailed description of Mrs Saunders, down to the shape of her jaw. He dropped a florin into the outstretched palm. It seemed an overly generous amount to me. Then the boy was gone, just as he had arrived, quickly and silently.

"And when do you propose we venture into Bohemia?"

Holmes reached for another cigarette.

"Tomorrow night if all goes well. A curious thing happened at Cavendish Square this morning. The maid showed me into a drawing room where I awaited Sir Robert. As I wandered about examining the furnishings, the gewgaws and the books on the shelves I heard a distinct ticking from inside the wall, like a timepiece. Have you an idea what that was?"

"Can't say I do. Very rum."

"The deathwatch beetle, Watson. An insect regarded by many as the harbinger of doom."

Upon my return I sat up late pondering the case, if it was in fact a case. Something seemed awry. Over the many years that I had known Holmes I had often been confused by his reasoning or his strange antics. Ultimately he would be proved correct. What was unintelligible became clear. It was his genius alone that illuminated the darkness. This ability had made him famous. It might very well have been the same on this occasion, and I with my befuddled intellect could not see what he saw, but my intuition, which Holmes scorned, told me otherwise. The case seemed to be running in reverse. Instead of approaching clarity it was becoming ever more obscure as it progressed.

The following evening, after I had closed my practice for the day I took my revolver from the desk drawer, cleaned it and loaded it with bullets. I then went to Baker Street to meet Holmes as arranged. He seemed in fine fettle and not the least bit apprehensive about walking into a trap.

"I visited my brother Mycroft at his club today and put the case to him."

"What opinion did he have?"

Mycroft was a man of high erudition and intelligence, which Holmes with unaccustomed modesty stated was greater than his own. He would seek his opinion from time to time when a particularly vexing problem arose. Unlike his brother, Mycroft was a man with no affinity for physical action. He spent his time between the Foreign Office and his club a few doors away, the Diogenes Club, an establishment that catered to gentlemen who eschewed conversation.

"He suggested that I keep in mind the theories of Thomas Bayes, namely Inverse Probability."

I had no skill for mathematics and was unaware of such a theory.

"You will have to educate me on that subject, Holmes."

"There is not time enough for a lengthy explication, but in short one assigns a probability value to unknown quantities, say nought or one, and then adjusts the values as the quantities become known. One refers backwards from effects to causes."

" I see."

"There are a lot of quantities unknown at present, Watson, but we must set forth. I received intelligence from my young spies that the address is indeed bonafide. The inhabitant is an artist by the name of Lawrence Wheeler. They saw no sign of our Bohemian, though they did tell me that they saw the Prince of Wales arrive in a nondescript hansom cab in the company of two questionable women."

"The Prince of Wales? That is highly unlikely."

"True. In their ignorant zeal they may well have mistaken him for another gentleman, but I think we have come across a bawdy house, Watson."

We made our way to Cleveland Street on foot. It was a foggy night and the gaslights glowed in dim, caliginous circles. Our footsteps rang hollow in the streets. We walked mostly in silence, there were few others abroad. When we reached our destination, Holmes rapped sharply on the door with his cane. There was some delay before the door was eventually opened and a portly man stood in the frame. His frock coat was faded and shabby, some of the stitching beginning to fray. His cheeks bristled with unruly bushes of whiskers. He surveyed us with suspicion and undisguised contempt.

"You are who?"

"I beg your pardon?" Said I.

"Wheeler Mr with speak to wish we." Holmes enjoined with fluency.

"You with off be," the man croaked as he slammed the door shut in our faces.

"What an unpleasant fellow. Is that affectation or lunacy, Holmes?"

"Affectation indubitably. As I said, everything here is done by design."

I felt the weight of the revolver in my pocket. Faint light shone through the curtained windows above us. It was a strange and anticlimactic outcome. A creeping lassitude subsumed me and chilled me to the bone. Holmes was silent and seemed indecisive. We wandered a little further down the street and waited, for what I know not.

The silence was suddenly broken by the sound of hooves on cobbles and an undertaker's carriage pulled by two black horses turned the corner and thundered down Cleveland Street at breakneck speed. I saw the driver hunched in his seat, a scarf tightly wound around his face, the reins in one gloved hand, a whip in the other. The carriage came to a halt outside the door from which we had recently been refused. We approached, Holmes with an enraptured and crazed look in his eye. The door swung open, and light spilled on to the pavement. A few words were exchanged but they were muffled and indeterminate. Three men left the building and climbed into the carriage. Then it was gone, its wheels splashing us with mud as it passed. The door it had obscured was closed firmly again as if it had never been opened. Stillness and quiet returned. Without speaking we both knew that there was nothing further to be accomplished and we made our uneasy way back to Baker Street.

I stayed in my old room that night, turning in upon arrival as neither of us was in the mood for conversation. When I awoke Holmes was gone. I suspected he had been up all night, as was his wont. I ordered some breakfast and Mrs Hudson brought in eggs with rashers of bacon and piping hot coffee. I had a remarkable hunger and felt much improved from the repast. After breakfast I had just sat back with the day's newspapers and one of Holmes' cigars when he slipped into the room. He was wearing a disguise and looked quite the convincing dandy with a purple velveteen jacket and a rumpled silk cravat, a wide-brimmed hat set at a jaunty angle. The image was marred by his state of dishevelment.

"You were back at Cleveland Street I presume? Did you learn anything new?"

"The facts change as I gather them. I am undone, Watson."

"Let me have Mrs Hudson bring you some breakfast. She is top notch today. Afterwards a hot bath will do you good."

"Not at present."

He turned and stumbled into his room. I glimpsed his face. Not even in his deepest depression had I ever seen Holmes with such an expression, a mask of abject desolation. I became alarmed, and going to his door called out to him but he gave no response. I put my ear to the door and heard him fumbling in his medicine cabinet and then the sound of him slumping into a chair. I knew exactly what he was doing. He was injecting himself with cocaine. As a medical man I could not condone this foul habit of his but I could understand it. When he was involved in a case he existed in a high state of stimulation. It was often between cases when his mind was not operating at such a level that he tended to lapse into depression and would resort to the drug as a means, I believe, of regaining the lost stimulation. This circumstance was different. He was involved in a case and would usually not feel the need to take cocaine. My concern grew steadily and I felt a sickness in the stomach.

I sat back down in a quandary until moments later I was up again, pounding on his door.

"Holmes?"

There was still no reply. I paced around the room until I could bear it no longer. I returned to his door and tried the handle but it was locked, so I forced entry. Holmes was lying on the floor. He was unresponsive but still conscious. Mrs Hudson, who had no doubt heard the commotion came fussing into the room. I told her to go back downstairs in no short order. I needed to devote my full attention to Holmes and could tolerate no distraction.

I raised him on to the bed and checked his pulse. It was normal, as was his breathing. A thorough examination convinced me that he was in no immediate danger.

I rang for Mrs Hudson, apologised for my curtness and had her send a message boy to my wife, explaining the situation and to my neighbour requesting that he should cover my practice for the day. That being done I remained by my friend's bedside.

For six weeks Holmes suffered from severe brain fever. I visited him daily, administering doses of laudanum to calm his anxiety as the need arose. This was a double blow, witnessing the sufferings of my dear friend and at the same time as his doctor searching for a cure I was not confident I would find. It caused me to doubt my abilities and I often wondered whether he would not be better served by an alienist. I was also in a state of dread that it might devolve upon me to have to commit him to a lunatic asylum.

Thankfully Holmes recovered and we were once more able to engage in meaningful conversation. He never, however, quite regained his former self. He was as intelligent as ever but in some way humble. I thought at first that this was an effect of the illness and would pass with time but it never did. In fact as the weeks went by I realised how profoundly he had changed. He no longer had any interest in pursuing his former work and as far as I know has not taken on a case since. He never mentioned this most recent case, which I call the Bohemian Adventure. Instead he talked of subjects in which he had previously shown no interest, such as horticulture and spiritualism.

After about a year, Holmes gave up the lodging we had long shared on Baker Street, a place I hold so dear in my memory.

He moved out of London and took up residence in Essex. Alas, our friendship waned. I wrote to him several times, thinking to go up and visit him, but he never responded. I do get a yearly note on the occasion of my birthday, so he has not forgotten me completely.

I often puzzle over the Bohemian Adventure. It sometimes keeps me up at night. On occasion I see the case merely as an outward expression of the onset of his illness, where seemingly inconsequential events had such a profound effect but there is an ambiguity to the whole thing that leaves me unconvinced. Holmes hated ambiguity. I remember those strange words he had uttered on that fateful morning, something to the effect that facts are changed by gathering them. It seems so paradoxical. Facts are after all the unblemished units of truth. How could they change and still remain facts? Would it not be a case of the facts being proved false? They could not then be considered factual. I have the sense though that this is not what he meant. I recall his face in a spasm of absolute horror. It is something I can never forget. He had told me he was undone. What could have been the cause? It was not physical trauma, my examination of him at the time had confirmed that. Then it must have been something mental. He had the look of a man lost to the point of no return and aware of it, a man whose every tenet of existence had been swept away, who had become a mere fiction to himself. What did Holmes discover there in Cleveland Street while I was sleeping? When he said that facts changed when you gather them, did he mean that he was influencing the case by investigating it? Then logic, at which he was so adept, and by which he had always governed his life would have become nothing more than a chimera. That would be a devastating realisation. These are heady thoughts indeed.

Yet there were indisputable facts about the case. We had been visited by the so-called Mrs Saunders, there was a fine carriage in the street, she had requested a cigar. I had witnessed this all myself. If Holmes had been speaking correctly, with full sanity and not from febrile imagination when he told me he was being manipulated, then his enemy had managed to finish him off, to neutralise him, in effect kill him without committing a single crime. It was devilishly ingenious.

John H. Watson, MD.
Camberwell, 1909

Meanwhile, on board the Calypso

I found a novel on a chair in a hotel—a well worn paperback with a coffee stain on the cover.

Little did I know then, the effect it was about to have on me.

A note fell out of the book as I picked it up—a scrap of paper upon which was written: "It's going to be Malta. Dennis."

What was going to be Malta? And who was Dennis? I imagined a man in his fifties, with hair the colour of straw.

The first unusual thing about the book was its copyright year. It was listed as 2735. The publisher, or author had chosen not to use the Gregorian calendar for some reason. It was obviously based on another system.

Aside from the date, everything else looked normal—the name of the book, the author, and the statement that any reference to real people, places and events was coincidental. It made me think of a person standing in a court of law, one hand on a venerated object—"I swear not to tell the truth, none of it, and nothing but lies."

On a whim I subtracted the current year from the date listed in the book. The result was 735—quite close to the year that Rome was supposedly founded in 753 BC, when wolves still suckled orphans.

If they were using the Roman calendar—*ab urbe condita*—and the date listed in the book was 2735, then it had been published in 1982. I was getting somewhere. The note from Dennis looked much more recent. The crispness of the paper and the fresh ink suggested it could have been placed in the book within the last few days. Dennis might still be in the hotel.

I went out to the terrace and sat at a table overlooking Lago Maggiore. The view was beautiful and deeply satisfying. The clouds hung motionless like statues. The sky and the water were separated by countless shades of green. The mountains waited at the edge of the lake. It was good to see things from a distance.

"Might I have a word with you?" A man had come up behind me.

Could this be Dennis? If so, he was not the way I had pictured him. He was short and slim, with dark hair and thick glasses. His eyes had a cold purity despite their myopic condition.

"There's been a misunderstanding."

He was working for a bureaucrat. That's what his eyes told me. A lackey who never felt responsibility for anything he did. Instinctively, I felt uncooperative.

"I see. So that would explain why I don't know what you're talking about."

He paused. I watched him as he considered for a moment what he could reveal.

"Have you been in the hotel long?"

"What hotel?"

There was a trace of a smile on his humourless lips.

"Let's not play games."

"Let's not. You can start by telling me who you are and what you want from me."

"I know this may seem unusual to you, but there is more going on at the moment than you're aware of. Does the number two thousand seven hundred and thirty-five mean anything to you?"

He was obviously after the book I had found but didn't want to mention it in case it was not me who had found it. He would be studying me for a reaction that would tell him I recognised the number.

"No. Why?"

He gave me a look of resignation like someone who had just lost a chess piece.

"Well, I am no doubt mistaken. I'm sorry to have bothered you. I do hope you enjoy the rest of your stay."

There was menace in his voice.

I knew then that I had to read this book. I just couldn't be seen reading it. The world was an odd place. I'd come to Locarno for a holiday, to go to the film festival and just to relax but now everything was veering off in another direction. It was a good thing I'd been looking at the lake, otherwise I might have had it on the table when he crept up on me. It was in the pocket of my jacket.

After that I went up to my room for some privacy. As soon as I opened the door I knew someone had been there, and not the maid. There was no evidence of a search—everything was neatly in its place, but I could sense an intrusion.

I pulled open the drawer of the bedside table. There was a book in it, with some loose change and my watch. I preferred not to wear my watch, not wishing to become a prisoner of time, but I always kept it with me as it had belonged to my grandfather.

Everything I had put in the drawer was still there but the book was in a slightly different position. I could remember the angle the spine had made with the side of the drawer. Someone had picked it up and then replaced it, though not exactly in the same position—a professional but not of the highest order.

That evening I went down to the bar, thinking I'd have a quick drink and then go into the town for another. There was a woman sitting alone at the end of the room, a Marlene Dietrich kind of woman. This had to be a set up, a honey trap. She kept glancing over, inviting me to make a move. I drained my glass and left the hotel. These people were relentless.

I walked around the town and treated myself to a meal in an expensive restaurant and then visited a couple of bars. I liked Locarno. I'd been there a few times as a child and liked it then too. We used to stay at a hotel a bit like the one I was in now. I remembered that the owner had a son, who must have been about twenty, though he looked older to me—maybe twenty was old in those days. He spent his time fucking the guests and doing heroin. He seemed nice enough to me. Everyone was nice then.

I was on my way back to the hotel, when two men came up behind me, one on each side. They pulled my jacket up over my head and bundled me into a car. It was so quick I barely knew what was happening. Then I was sitting in the back, wedged between them. One of them brandished a syringe. He brushed aside my jacket and plunged it into my arm.

When I came round I was in a small room, naked and tied to a chair. A man sat across from me. The room was brightly lit. There was a table between us and he had a sheaf of papers in his hand.

"Tell me why you are here."

I felt groggy and the room was moving. It must have been a residual effect from the drug they had given me.

"I think you'd be the one to answer that."

He thumbed through his papers, then looked up at me.

"You'd be wise not to play the fool."

"I'm on holiday. I came here for the film festival."

"You can do better than that. Tell me about Dennis. Where is he?"

"I don't know anyone called Dennis."

"Yet he sent you a message." He held up the piece of paper that had fallen from the book.

"That doesn't mean I know him."

"Tell me about Malta."

"It's an island in the Mediterranean, strategically important once. Perhaps it still is. I don't know much about it. Then there's the Maltese Falcon, the film with Humphrey Bogart. I think the Knights of St John paid for their lease of the island with a Maltese falcon every year. Maybe that's where the idea for the film, or the book came from."

"You're wasting my time. And yours. Flippancy wont help you."

Just then the door opened and he got up from the table and conversed with someone I couldn't see. I was unable to hear what they were saying. Then he returned.

"I'll give you one more chance. Come clean."

"Come clean with what? I can't answer questions I don't understand."

"All right then."

He got up again and went back to the door. The two men who had kidnapped me off the street came in. They must have been waiting outside the whole time. They untied me and took me from the room. It was then that I realised we were on a boat.

They led me up to the deck. I saw a plank extending out over the dark water. One of them had drawn a gun.

"Go on, then."

Better to walk the plank than get shot, I thought, so I tumbled into the lake.

The cold water revived me and I was able to swim away from the boat, underwater at first to avoid detection. The lake was big and how I managed to reach the shore I don't know. But I had survived and wasn't the suicide they'd intended, or the delinquent tourist who had accidentally drowned himself. Now, of course, I would have to deal with the Swiss police, who wouldn't take kindly to a naked man wandering around Locarno.

I lay on the bank listening to the birds. All of this had happened because I'd picked up a book from a chair. I couldn't remember the name of the author but I hadn't forgotten the title—*Meanwhile, on board the Calypso.*

And I never even read it.

Arborist, Ventriloquist, Comedian

Three men got lost—an arborist, a ventriloquist and a comedian.

The arborist, naturally enough, had lost his way in a forest. He had heard reports of a dendroglyph carved in an ancient tree by unknown people. The location he had been given was vague. After hours walking under the dense canopy he no longer knew where he was. Night was falling.

He had found the ancient tree many times without knowing it. The tree had fallen and the glyph was either facing the ground, or had rotted away. He had passed by this tree, walked around it and had even stood on it. The irony escaped him.

He sat down on it. With the onset of night came the dawn of hopelessness. He knew he could do nothing until the next day. Even then he might not find his way out. He was foolish to have come alone, though self recrimination wouldn't help him now.

Perhaps the people of the forest would find him. He remembered reading about a young missionary, who had set off alone, brimming with zeal and righteousness. He was going to help these people by bringing them knowledge of God's love. He rowed across a river to an island and they killed him within two minutes of reaching the shore. He hadn't even opened his mouth to speak to them. He hadn't even seen them.

What would he be going back to if he ever found his way?

The ventriloquist had lost his voice. It wasn't due to laryngitis. He was able to speak but not in his own voice. He could only speak in the voice of his sidekick dummy, who was called Ivan, and who had Tourette Syndome.

The comedian was a flibbertigibbet run dry. It was perhaps a case when having nothing to say finally extinguished the need to talk.

That about sums it up.

One of Three

The trouble started when he went for a walk. Or perhaps it had started earlier with the cup of coffee he drank just before going out. It wasn't so much the coffee as the milk, but that had not seemed important at the time.

It was cold outside. The residue of a snowstorm lingered along the sides of the road. The potholes were filled with icy water. There was no one about. Even the birds had gone.

As he turned up Whitehead Road he thought that were it not for the occasional low rumble of distant traffic he could be walking in any era. This was the potentiality of time travel—that sense of otherness in a familiar place. The desire to build a machine to do the job was just a vestige of industrial capitalism. There was no need for strange alloys and glowing control panels. It only required perception.

He was coming to his favourite stretch of the road where it bent like an S, past the decayed tennis court. There was a gentle upward slope that curved slightly to the right and blocked his vision—just long enough to delay the onset of pleasure for half a second. This part of the road had a pungent lack of time. It was appealing all year long—from the blossoms of the mountain laurel to the dead leaves and finally the ice.

There was an old culvert that he liked to stop and look at whenever he walked that way. It was a rectangular trough encased in bluestone that vanished beneath a driveway, but as he approached it he saw that he was not alone. Someone else was already there. A man stood looking at the stones. His clothing was eccentric—jodhpurs disappearing into knee-high boots and a military style coat of green tweed, open despite the cold, with no shirt beneath it. He looked like a modern version of a Cossack.

Timelessness contracted into the present with a jolt. His mood was tarnished. He never liked to meet other people while he was walking. They felt like trespassers, or poachers who stole away the mystery of his surroundings.

He regained his composure as he continued around the S-bend, alone again. The dry, wizened tangle of wild vines made scribbles against the cold sky. This section was short—too short. It was always a disappointment. He would have liked to walk on it for at least half an hour but it only took several minutes. He was soon in the woods, heading towards White Pines, the house that Ralph Whitehead had built for himself in 1902.

Then he saw the Cossack again, leaning on a boulder, smoking a cigarette. It came as a shock and his heart rate quickened.

How could this man be ahead of him when he had just left him behind? He could see his face but not his eyes. They were covered by a pair of blue mirrored sunglasses. In each lens was a distorted, minuscule version of himself. The Cossack leant back, nonchalantly smoking his cigarette. It was impossible to know what those eyes were looking at.

He was suddenly overcome with doubt. Everything seemed different—the light, the trees, the rocks. He felt as if he had become a figment of the landscape.

When he emerged from the trees at the Whitehead house, the Cossack was already there, peering into a window. It was strangely unsurprising to see him again. Three times was all it had taken for him to accept the impossible.

"Excuse me. Can you tell me how you've managed to stay ahead of me, when I've passed you twice?"

"If I could tell you that, I wouldn't be here."

"Where would you be then?"

"Somewhere else." He had a faint Irish accent. His face had a weather-beaten quality that suggested a tough life, even though he barely looked forty. Thick black hair brushed his shoulders. His eyes were still obscured.

"So it's not just me. You've noticed it too."

"I have. But the way I see it is that you're always behind me, no matter how many times you pass me by."

"Well, we're in the same place now."

They were standing at the front door of White Pines. It seemed a little too narrow for a building that size. It reminded him of an entrance to a tomb. There was a heaviness to the place, with its thick beams and dark siding. There was also the weight of history that had run its course—the aroma of absence. Once, this house had been the centre of a utopian community, humming with artists, potters and craftsmen. Ralph Whitehead had owned most of the mountain then. He had bought it with the profits from his father's mills in England. A catalytic spark of inspiration from William Morris had created this utopia. There had been parties and wealthy visitors. Furniture was built. Domestic servants were an acceptable necessity.

He tried the door. It was locked. It always was.

"What do you think is happening?"

"I don't think there's anything happening, Mister, that hasn't been happening for a long time already."

"I think there's something unusual going on."

"That's because you're one of three."

One of three. The way he said 'three' made it sound like 'tree', which was faintly amusing.

"Who are the other two, then?"

"Well one of them would be me. And the turd would be the both of us together."

The Right Moment

The moon was one hundred and seventy-two thousand eight hundred minutes away from fullness. It was to be a harvest moon, a circle aglow in cyclical time. Fields of wheat and grasses were drenched in its light, their stalks bent under its weight, caressed by a gentle breeze, their hairy ears full of grain and promise.

Bisecting the fields was a road that preferred to be a river. When the people who lived nearby were in their beds, distracted by dreams, the surface would melt and flow into the distance. As the solids became liquid, hundreds of fish, moments earlier only sleeping stones, now jumped and dived in the water with the sheer unconscious happiness of materialisation.

Through the course of the long night all the water in the river evaporated into steam and gas, rising ever upwards through the atmosphere to feed the hungry moon, greedy for affection and nourishment, lonely in the sky.

Long before the shadowed fields had turned gray-green and morning was not yet a thought, the residue of this feast fell back down and congealed again into the solid road, ready for the first foot and wheel. This whole process caused a peculiar vibration, which was the music of crickets and frogs.

The first feet to step on to the freshly hardened surface, now disappearing into forever, belonged to farmers, up at dawn, shouldering their scythes. The first wheels belonged to the cart they were dragging behind them. Their blades cut through the air to reach the stalks which they slashed and hewed, tying the fallen ones into great bundles, and tossing them on to the cart.

The fields of grain were soon to be pounded and ground to dust.

While the miller was grinding and the farmers were resting from their toil, either sleeping or drunk on an amber nectar that shimmered with vibrant bubbles, there was a man who had just turned twenty, wide awake and sober. He never worked in the fields, as the farmers would have nothing to do with him. He had a shock of hair which fell across one eye and caused him to flip his head back from time to time. People found it disconcerting. The threat of repetitive movement in random bursts troubled them deeply and so they left him alone with his thoughts. Only one person did not avoid him, and that was an old woman, who was blind and could not see him toss his head.

She was wise but lonely, everyone she had loved had long since departed. Her wisdom was a stream with banks of stones, some covered by slick green algae just below the surface, which was never in the same place twice. No one appreciated this wisdom except the young twenty-year-old man. They alleviated their loneliness with friendship.

The old woman told the young man about the right moment. He decided then that he would find it. This was not an easy task as there were so many moments. The first step would be to discover what a moment actually was, otherwise he would be stumbling in the dark. The old woman never stumbled even though she could not see. She made him scones and presented them to him on a plate covered with a cloth of faded stripes reminiscent of summers long passed. Sometimes she would turn him away from her door without explanation. Whenever this happened he would wander through the fields, listening to the flies.

She had said that although there were many moments, usually only one was correct and it changed everyday. On rare occasions there could be two or three in a day. The matter was further complicated because the moment he was looking for was not the same for everybody. The shifting uncertainty excited him. She had sometimes described the right moment as a gateway—two heavy wooden doors supported by stone columns that were three times the height of a man. The doors were decorated with symbols made from beaten metal and nailed in place. They formed ideograms, which were thought to describe the pleasures of the right moment and all its possible variations of bliss.

Success depended upon reading this script. It was more important than crossing the threshold. Any fool could go through a door. It was second nature. People had been doing it for years.

Instinctively he knew that the writing on the doors had to be read by touch as well as sight, for the message was emotional and could only be understood through physical sensation. He would let his hands run gently across the raised symbols, his fingertips receiving details of such delicacy they could not be perceived by his imagination. The correct moment must be tactile. While his hands brushed the surface he would let his eyes flit over it without focusing, experiencing only wholeness, but first he had to find it.

Twenty-one years had passed since he had turned twenty. All that time must have been comprised of many moments, none of them the right one. He berated himself because he had not yet been able to decide what exactly constituted a moment. There had been distractions, red herrings, false starts, disasters and loose ends. Still he did not know. He had raised his foot to take the first step and after all those years had not put it down to take the second.

The fields in which the farmers had swung their scythes had become a town. According to the old woman, this was the result of one thing being placed upon another. He remembered everything she said, though he could never be sure what she had meant, or how she had meant it.

Those doors with their mysterious script suggested the gates of an ancient walled city, which had gone the way of empires—destroyed by war or time, or by the earth itself. Nothing remained but the entrance to nowhere, or the exit. It was possible that there had been other gates when the city had existed, one for each cardinal point. Now only one remained. But was this city Mesopotamian or Mesoamerican?

Time had its own geography. The moment was a place. The quest to find it bordered on futility. It had to be approached without the usual rational comprehension of things. Objectivity and subjectivity needed to merge and become each other. That required self-knowledge. He had looked deeply into himself and seen nothing there. The idea of selfhood, seemingly so foundational, was just a convenience, a tool for discerning the differences of perceived objects.

The other foot was coming down, displacing particles of giant rocks eroded into sand by the weather over unquantifiable numbers of seconds arranged as aeons. There were no creeping vines, no giant rodents, no sloths meditating among branches, no birds which saturated the eyes with colour. This meant the city had been Mesopotamian.

The ground was strewn with dice, pockmarked by invisible forces and so small their existence was uncertain. Among them were the bones of dinosaurs, bleached by the sun which gave them the impression of whiteness. But the white was yellow or ochre, in various shades of density. It was a whiteness that contained all colour. The dinosaurs had been drinking at the shore of a large lake when time had moved on.

The wind came through the dunes carrying pages torn from bibles. It spoke in the voice of the succubus, Meridiana, calling out to travellers blinded by the swirling sands. Supine from her beauty they would love her in their dreams and she would bestow febrile and unimagined delights in exchange for the semen she needed to survive, as was the way of mammals and demons. Her dainty feet bore the talons of a bird. The incubus was jealous.

The wind departed suddenly, impatient and bored with the dunes, wishing to visit somewhere else. The grains of sand it had lifted were now free to fall back down to the earth where they belonged. These events—the forces and the landscapes, the clearing of the sandstorm, the voices of demons, the hypnosis of pleasures, the bones, the sky and the planets beyond it, the empty spaces—all of it was an expression of love, declared in one exhalation, a love both divided and whole.

When the air cleared and the sand settled, the right moment was revealed against the sky, two columns the height of three men and between them the two wooden doors—the gateway to a city that no longer existed. The doorway had been liberated from its original purpose and was able to assume a loftier significance. It could be inspected from both sides without the encumbrance of entry and exit, of acceptance and denial. The symbols gave themselves up to the fingers that tickled them, excited and relaxed, basking in the pleasure of touch. In their abandon they felt generous and allowed their meaning to be understood.

On the doors was written:

The moon was one hundred and seventy-two thousand eight hundred minutes away from fullness...

The End

About the Author

Tom Newton lives in Woodstock, New York with his wife and daughter. His novella *Warfilm* was published by Bloomsbury in 2015. He is the author of *Seven Cries of Delight and Other Stories* (Recital Publishing, 2019), *Voyages to Nowhere: Two Novellas* (Recital Publishing, 2021) and *Fabian: A Cubist Biography* (Recital Publishing, 2025). He spent many years working in the film industry, while pursuing his interests in music and sound engineering.

A Request

If you enjoyed this book, its author and publisher would be grateful if you would post a short (or long) review on the website where you bought the book and/or on *goodreads.com* or other book review sites.

Other Books from Recital Publishing

The Eleventh Commandment by Rhys Hughes
Fabian: A Cubist Biography by Tom Newton
Three Roman Pennies by M.M.B. Higham
A Book with No Author by Brent Robison
Overlook: A Rock & Roll Fable by Paul Smart
The Berserkers by Vic Peterson
The House of the Seven Heavens by Mark Morganstern
Voices in the Dirt: Stories by Ian Caskey
Our Lady of the Serpents by Petrie Harbouri
Voyages to Nowhere: Two Novellas by Tom Newton
The Lame Angel by Alexis Panselinos
The Joppenbergh Jump by Mark Morganstern
Ponckhockie Union by Brent Robison
Seven Cries of Delight and Other Stories by Tom Newton
Saraceno by Djelloul Marbrook
Dancing with Dasein by Mark Morganstern
The Principle of Ultimate Indivisibility by Brent Robison

And please check out **The Strange Recital**, a podcast about
fiction that questions the nature of reality.

www.ingramcontent.com/pod-product-compliance
Lightning Source LLC
Chambersburg PA
CBHW030004010826
48973CB00009B/2662